Ernestine & Amanda

Summer Camp: Ready or Not!

Ernestine & Amanda

SUMMER CAMP Ready or Not!

Sandra Belton

SIMON & SCHUSTER BOOKS FOR YOUNG READERS

SIMON & SCHUSTER BOOKS FOR YOUNG READERS
An imprint of Simon & Schuster Children's Publishing Division
1230 Avenue of the Americas, New York, New York 10020

Book design by Heather Wood • The text for this book is set in Goudy Old Style.
Printed and bound in the United States of America
10 9 8 7 6 5 4 3 2 1 First Edition

Library of Congress Cataloging-in-Publication Data
Belton, Sandra.
Ernestine & Amanda : summer camp, ready or not! / by Sandra Belton.
p. cm.
Summary: Ernestine and Amanda, two African-American girls growing up in the 1950s, go away to different summer camps and make discoveries about what they can expect from themselves and other people. ISBN 0-689-80846-1
[1. Camps—Fiction. 2. Afro-Americans—Fiction.] I. Title.
PZ7.B4197Er 1997 [Fic]—dc20 96-4144

For phyllis barbee beane,
who knew it first
and is partial to the second!
Thank you, dear sister-friend.

Ernestine & Amanda

Summer Camp: Ready or Not!

Ernestine & Amanda

"HELLO, CAN I speak to Amanda?"

"This is Amanda. Hello, Ernestine."

"Amanda! You don't sound like yourself."

"Who do I sound like?"

"You sound kinda like you have, um, an accent or somethin'. You just don't sound like you, that's all."

"Well, you sound like you."

"That's how I'm supposed to sound."

"Look, Ernestine, did you call me up to have an argument?"

"No. I called to invite you to my birthday party. It's gonna be next Saturday."

"Splashing!"

"What?"

"I said, 'Splashing.'"

"Girl, whadda you talkin' about? I didn't say nothin'

about going swimming. Where would we be going swimming? It's a *party*. A party at my house."

"For your information, Ernestine, 'splashing' means, like, 'terrific.' You know, 'great idea.' Stuff like that. People say it all the time."

"*I* never heard anybody say it before."

"So? That doesn't mean it's not somethin' people say. Anyhow, what you've never heard of would probably fill a zillion encyclopedias."

"Look, Amanda, do you want to come to my party or not?"

"Like I said, 'Splashing!' And just to make doubly sure you understand, that means 'yes.' What time does it start?"

"Three o'clock. And *don't* bring a bathing suit."

"Very funny."

"I just want to make doubly sure you know we won't be going swimmin'."

"For your information, I went swimming so much this summer it was beginning to get on my nerves. We swam every day at my camp."

"And, for your information, so did we. Sometimes I went swimming *twice* a day."

"You'll have to tell me about *your* camp some time."

"I will. And you'll have to tell me about *yours*...."

Week 1

1 Ernestine

"MAMA, I DON'T *want* to go away to camp!"

I hated the way my voice sounded. I was almost whining! I tried to talk regular, but the whining kept popping in.

"How come Jazz can't go? She *said* she wanted to go to camp. I *never* said I did."

Mama wouldn't look at me. She kept on looking through her purse. I wanted to snatch it out of her hand and make her look at me.

"Mama? Do you hear what I'm sayin'?"

Mama turned her head just enough to look at me out the corner of her eye. I could tell from the look that how I was feeling had sneaked into my voice. I figured I'd better keep talking.

"Mama, you said you were going to teach me how to sew this summer, remember? How can we do that if I'm away at camp?" The whining was gone from my voice; now I sounded like my sister, Jazz, when she does her icky fake sweet voice. But I had no choice. I just *had* to convince Mama.

"Huh, Mama? How can I learn to sew if I'm away at camp? And you said that if I wanted to have some skirts like the kind Alicia wears that maybe I could learn to make them this summer. Remember, Mama? That's what you said. And if I'm away at camp you won't be able to teach me and I won't be able to make them and—"

"Ernestine! Please hush!"

Mama's voice came out so loud I stepped back without meaning to. My ankle bone hit against the corner of her bed, but I didn't scream "ouch" like I wanted to. I didn't say anything.

Mama looked at me and then turned her head away. Her face looked real funny, almost like she was ready to cry. The look made me feel even worse than I was already feeling.

"Mama," I said, and started walking around the bed to get on the same side as her.

Mama started shaking her head back and forth and held up her hand like she does when she wants us to leave her alone. Then she turned around to look at me again. Her face looked practically regular. I felt like saying "whew" out loud.

"Look, Ernestine," Mama said, "going away to camp is a *good* thing. There's no reason for you to go on like this. You're acting as if you're being punished, and I want it to stop. Right now. Daddy and I want...this is something special for you...."

Mama's voice kinda broke, and she turned away again. I

wanted to say something, but I couldn't think of anything. I figured Mama wanted me to say she was right and that I was glad I was supposed to go away to camp. But I couldn't say that. It would be an outright lie. It *wasn't* okay. Going to camp would be awful. Terrible. Hideous. Horrendous.

A picture of Mrs. Lawson, the fifth-grade teacher I had last year, popped into my mind while I stood there thinking of every word I could that meant "awful." I could hear her saying, "Do a synonym study, Ernestine." The picture made me want to laugh and cry at the same time.

I figured maybe that was the way Mama felt. Her eyes looked like they had tears in them at the same time her mouth was smiling. Standing there looking at her, I knew I couldn't stay quiet. I *had* to say something, even if it didn't come out right and got me in trouble. I took a deep breath.

"Mama, I'm not glad I'm going to camp and that's the truth but I don't want you or Daddy to feel bad and think I'm not thankful for all the things you do for us but I just thought that maybe it would be better for Jazz to go to camp because she really wants to go and maybe she could take my place and while she's there I could be home and we could spend time together while I learn how to sew."

Everything popped out in one long sentence that didn't end until I ran out of breath. It must have been okay though, because when I finished Mama looked at me and started shaking her head again. Only this time she was smiling all the way. Then I knew she didn't mean for me to leave her alone.

"Ernestine," she said, still shaking her head, "you are something else. Baby, you *are* going to camp, but we'll talk about that later. You, me, and Daddy. We'll sit down together and get it all straightened out."

Mama put her arm around my shoulder. "You'll see, sweetheart. Going to camp won't be so bad, I promise. And part of the fun will be getting ready. Like going downtown and picking out things you'll need. That'll be fun, don't you think?"

I just moved my head to say "yes." I could tell Mama was feeling okay again, but I had talked out. For now. I figured I'd have more luck when we got together to talk about it like she said we would do. Maybe I'd tell Jazz to be there, too. Since she wanted to go to camp, she could help me convince Mama and Daddy that she should be the one to go and not me.

Usually I don't want Jazz in on anything. Eight-year-olds are a real pain most of the time, and my sister Jazz is one practically all the time. To make it worse, she's also peculiar. That's the word my best friend, Clovis, used for Jazz when he saw her in the costume she made for herself last Halloween. And the name "peculiar" fits her just perfectly.

When Jazz came bouncing out of the house on Halloween, ready to go trick-or-treat with us, Clovis looked at her and said, "Jazz, what are you supposed to be?" That's what anybody would have asked after taking a look at Jazz. Her entire body was wrapped in a yellow sheet. Even her arms and hands were wrapped inside. Her feet were in a brown paper bag that was taped all the way around her legs with some of Daddy's silver electrical tape. She had painted her face yellow and had taped a big yellow construction paper hat to her head. The hat was in the shape of a cone. The top part of it was painted to look like a mountain peak, except that it was colored black.

Jazz hopped over to Clovis. "Whadda you mean, 'supposed to be'?" she said, sticking her pointy-top head in Clovis's face. "I'm a *pencil*, and if you don't watch out I'll put my eraser feet in your face and rub you out!" Jazz howled like she was dressed up to be some kind of wild animal instead of a pencil, and then she bounced on down the porch steps. Looking at her from behind, we saw a paper bag taped to her back with Jazz's writing on it. It said: THANKS FOR THE TREATS!

"Your sister is one peculiar kid," Clovis said.

Jazz is practically *more* than peculiar. She won't even answer when someone calls her by her real name, which is Jessie Louise. Jazz is the name she calls herself because she loves jazz music so much. And even though she's only eight she knows almost as much about it as Daddy and Uncle J. B. Sometimes when they're sitting in the living room and listening to some of Daddy's records, Jazz starts "doin' her thing." That's what Uncle J. B. says when Jazz puts on a show. Uncle J. B. says Jazz can "bebop with the best of them," whatever that means. But it must be something good because whenever Jazz is in there doing her thing, Daddy and Uncle J. B. carry on like she's doing magic.

I figured magic would be what I'd need to get out of going to camp, so I went to find Jazz right after I left Mama's room. On the way downstairs, I bumped into my brother, Marcus, who was coming up the stairs.

"Where you off to, Miss Famous Lady?" Marcus asked. He's been calling me that ever since the recital my music teacher had last spring. He said I was important now because I had appeared on a stage.

"Marcus, I gotta find Jazz," I said.

"What'd she do now?"

"How come you think she did something?"

"Why else would you want to find your little sister, whom you love so much?" Marcus had the look on his face he gets when he says one thing and means another.

"I do love Jazz," I said. "I just don't like her most of the time. But today I do."

"Hope you get what you want," Marcus said. He started walking again, but I stood in his way.

"Marcus." I started whispering so Mama wouldn't hear me. "Jazz can help me get outta goin' to camp. Camp would be hideous for me but not for Jazz. She *wants* to go. Honest. What I think we oughta do is—"

I didn't get a chance to finish. Marcus grabbed my hand. He turned from the upstairs direction and started in the downstairs direction, pulling me with him. When we got to the bottom, he pulled me into the kitchen. Then he started whispering, too.

"Look, Ernestine," he said, "don't start carrying on about camp. This isn't a good time for any of us to rock the boat."

"Whadda you talkin' about?" I said, trying to pull away. Marcus was practically squeezing my arm off.

Marcus dropped my arm and looked at me without saying anything. Then he put his arm around my shoulders.

"Ernestine, you're going to be eleven at the end of the summer, and I think that makes you old enough to know what's going on and to handle it after you know."

Marcus looks more like Mama than me or Jazz. While he was standing there with his arm around my shoulders and talking right in my face, I started seeing Mama's face the way it had looked while we were talking in her room. It gave me a funny feeling. It told me that something really *was* wrong.

"What's wrong, Marcus? What's happening?"

"Mama and Daddy don't want you and Jazz to know about this yet, so you gotta promise not to say anything until they tell you themselves. Okay?"

"Promise." My voice sounded small. I cleared my throat so it wouldn't make that whining sound again.

"Dad's losing his job."

After the words popped out of Marcus's mouth, both of us just stood there. I think Marcus was waiting for me to say something at the same time I was waiting for him to.

"Dad and Mom are trying to figure something out," Marcus said, "and they probably will. But in the meantime, they got as much on their plate as they can deal with. None of us should do anything to add more. That means none of us—Jazz, me, and *you*." Marcus pointed his finger at me when he said the last part.

"How come you think *I* would do something to make them feel worse, Marcus?" I said, pointing my finger back at him.

Marcus wrapped his hand around my finger. His voice got soft. "I don't think you'd do anything on purpose, little sis," he said, "but you gotta understand that making a fuss about going to camp won't exactly help matters."

Marcus held on to my finger and used it to twirl my hand and arm back and forth. "Sending you to camp is part of their summer plan for you," he said, "just like sending Jazz somewhere else is their plan for her, and—"

"Where?" I cut in. "Where are they sending Jazz?"

He dropped my hand and shook his head. "I've already said enough, Ernestine. Mama and Dad are gonna talk to you soon enough." He pointed his finger at me again. "And you'd better not say one word about this talk we've had. Promise?"

"I promise."

"Look, I gotta go get ready. Madelyn asked me to take her somewhere, and if I don't hurry I'll be late." Marcus leaned over and whispered in my ear. "Stop looking like the world's gonna come to an end. Things'll work out."

I wanted to point my finger in Marcus's face and ask him how he figured he knew so much.

What do you know, Marcus? You're such a dummy you do anything some old girl tells you to do.

But I didn't say anything. I just stood there in the kitchen doorway and watched my brother run up the steps, two at a time.

The calendar our church sends out every year was swinging back and forth on the kitchen door. Marcus had bumped into it when he went flying out to get ready. I reached over to stop the calendar from swinging so it wouldn't tear off the nail. That's when I noticed the date. It was the first week of June. The first month of summer.

But I'm the biggest dummy of all. I thought this was gonna be a good summer, and it's gonna be the most horrendous summer of my whole entire life!

2 ❧ *Amanda*

EVERY YEAR I WAIT for summer more than I wait for Christmas. In the first place, my birthday is on the first official day of summer, which is June 21, even though everybody knows that summer *really* begins as soon as boring school lets out. And having a summer birthday is the best. It means being able to have an outdoor party and inviting as many people as you want.

Even though my birthday is the best day of any year, I had been trying *not* to think about it so much this year. I hadn't talked about it either. Usually I start giving hints to my parents in May so they won't have any trouble deciding what to get me for a present. But this year I hadn't said anything about my birthday to anybody in my family. Mostly because things had been really weird around our house, and May had been the weirdest month of all. That's when my sister, Madelyn, told me that our parents might be getting a separation.

When Madelyn first told me, I thought the inside of me was going to break into pieces. It was awful, awful, AWFUL! I couldn't talk to anybody about it, not even to Madelyn. Then, after she didn't say any more about it herself, I began to think maybe she had made a mistake. That maybe when Mother told her about the might-be-a-separation, Mother had been so upset, a separation was what she thought she wanted.

I really thought this after school finally let out for the summer. That's when Mother and Dad stopped arguing with each other so much. The best was that they also stopped yelling like they had been doing for months. The yelling had been the worst of all. They yelled at each other and sometimes even at us. It was TERRIBLE! But all the awful stuff had stopped, and lately things were almost like normal. The way they had been before my parents started being mad with each other all the time. Mother and Dad were acting almost like their old selves. Even Madelyn had stopped being so moody and was being her same old self—the self that really gets on my nerves.

My sister Madelyn was seventeen on her last birthday, and I'll be eleven on June 21. My godmother, Frankie, says that's why we have trouble getting along. "Because of the differences in your ages, you have different priorities," she said last week when she took me roller-skating. After she explained what "priorities" means, I knew she was right. Madelyn's priority is herself. She is so much her own priority, she makes a kissy face at herself every time she walks by a mirror. I can hardly believe it!

Marcus Harris is also Madelyn's priority. He's been her

boyfriend for almost a year. But Marcus graduated this May and will be going away to college in September, so Madelyn probably won't be *his* priority for long. Madelyn would probably follow Marcus to college if she could, but she can't because she still has two more years in high school. She'll probably pass out from loneliness when he leaves.

Marcus has a sister my same age, except I'll be eleven before she will. Her name is Ernestine. I know her because we take music lessons from the same teacher, Miss Clarice Elder. I used to think Ernestine was stuck up because of how good she plays the piano. She can even play songs she's never seen the music to. Stuff she's only heard. People call that being able to "play by ear."

Ernestine is okay, I guess, even though she's, well, actually she's a little fat. I used to call her Fatso, although I never said it to her face. That's not the reason I didn't particularly like her, but she's been fat the whole time I've known her.

Ernestine got very friendly with *my* good friend Alicia Raymond, who lives next door to me and takes music lessons from Miss Elder, too. For a while Alicia was mad at me because I didn't want to be around Ernestine. But everything's fine now, and since it's summer and we won't be taking music lessons for a while, it doesn't matter whether I like Ernestine or not because Ernestine won't be around much.

I was thinking about this while I cleaned up my room. Every Saturday Madelyn and I have to change our beds and dust and stuff like that before we can do any of the things we *want* to do. Madelyn has to vacuum both our rooms, and I have to take out all the trash. I was hurrying up to finish so I could go over to Alicia's house. I was going with her and her twin sister, Edna, to some kind of outdoor fair their mother's club was having to raise money. I had just finished making up my bed when Madelyn came in my room.

"Amanda?"

"Uh-uh," I said, shaking my head to mean "no." Madelyn had that I-want-you-to-do-something-for-me sound in her voice, and the only thing I was planning on doing was hurry up and leave.

"What are you talking about, 'uh-uh'?" Madelyn said. "I haven't asked you anything. All I did was say your name."

"Yeah, but I can tell you want something," I said, tossing my throw-pillows on my bed. "And whatever it is, I don't have time."

Madelyn acted like she hadn't heard me. She picked up the pillow I had thrown too far and sat on my just-made-up bed. "Amanda," she said, "we have to talk."

I hate it when people just keep on with whatever they're fixing to say or do no matter what. I hate it especially when my sister with all of her priorities does it.

"Didn't you hear what I said, Madelyn?" I snatched the pillow she had picked up off the floor and threw it again. This time it landed where it belonged. "I'm in a hurry. I have some place to go."

Madelyn kept sitting there, still acting like she hadn't heard a word I said. Except now, her eyes looked like they had tears in them. Weird.

"Amanda, please listen. You have to listen."

Madelyn's voice was beginning to sound teary. I sat down on the edge of the bed so I wouldn't be able to see her face. I hoped that not seeing her face would make the teary sound go away from her voice.

"Remember when I told you that Mother and Dad might be going to...ah, deciding to, um..."

Madelyn's teary voice started wobbling. I wanted to help her out, but I didn't know what I could say. Finally she cleared her throat and started again.

"Amanda, Mother and Dad have decided to separate... to live in separate places. Dad's gonna move out, and Mother will stay here with us."

Even though I tried really hard not to, I couldn't keep from remembering how it had been when Madelyn first talked about the might-be-a-separation. How I had felt tiny freezing-cold feet marching all through my body. It was a way I had never felt before and never ever *ever* wanted to feel again. But since Madelyn was back in my room, telling me the same thing again, I knew the terrible marching was going to start again.

But it didn't. The tiny cold feet weren't anywhere around. I didn't feel anything. Everything inside was empty.

"Amanda? Did you hear what I said?"

Madelyn's voice sounded okay again, so I thought the tears would be gone from her face and it would be safe now to look at her. But when I turned around to look at my sister I started feeling the tears. They were falling on my arms and hands. Then I got confused. Madelyn was sitting up near the head of my bed. Up by my pillows. I was sitting at the foot. How come I could feel her tears from so far away?

I don't remember Madelyn getting up or coming close to where I was. But suddenly there she was, with her arms around me. And the moving-everywhere tears were getting her dress wet. The same stupid tears that had wet up my arms and hands and my face. My tears.

Madelyn started rubbing my neck and back with her fingers. Her hand was warm and soft like her voice was when she whispered to me. "It's gonna be okay, Amanda. It hurts like crazy now, I know. But somehow it's gonna work out. It really will...."

I went with Madelyn when she went back to her room to get ready. Marcus had promised to take her someplace, she said. She wanted to know if I would be okay, and I said I would. I thought about teasing her and saying that I wouldn't want to keep her from one of her priorities, but I didn't.

I sat on Madelyn's bed while she fixed her hair. There were so many questions I wanted to ask, but I was afraid to. In the first place, I wasn't sure I wanted to know the answers. And what if the answers brought back the tiny freezing feet? But there was one thing I just had to ask, that I just had to know.

I looked in Madelyn's mirror to see her face. "Madelyn ...ah, when?"

She stopped pinning up her hair and turned around to look at me. "Soon. Before summer's over."

"Before my birthday?" I swallowed hard to keep the freezing feet from starting up.

Madelyn got up and came over to sit next to me on her bed. "No," she said. "I know it won't be before your birthday."

Madelyn took a long breath. Usually she does that when

something is getting on her nerves, but I knew the breath didn't mean that this time. It meant something, though, and I had to find out what it was.

"What, Madelyn? What else do you know?"

Madelyn took another breath before she told me. "Well...Amanda, before I tell you, you've got to swear you'll keep your mouth closed about this when you hear it from Mother. Do you swear?"

"I swear," I said. I crossed my heart with my right hand and held up my fingers so Madelyn could see they weren't crossed and would know that I was telling the truth.

"Well, they're sending you to camp so you'll be...ah, away from things while...well, you know."

"CAMP?" I couldn't believe it. While my parents were getting ready to wreck the rest of my life, I was going to have to go away to camp! To crummy Hilltop where all the kids we know go to camp. I just couldn't believe it!

"You'll be going to Hilltop, too, right? I won't have to go away to that crummy camp by myself, will I?"

Madelyn started getting that awful look on her face again. I turned my face away from hers.

"Amanda, I'm too old to go away to camp. Anyhow, I have a job this summer. We talked about it the other night at dinner. Remember?"

I didn't remember, but even if I had it didn't matter. *I* was still being sent away. To *camp*!

Madelyn put her hand on my shoulder. "But you're not going to Hilltop," she said.

"Whadda you mean 'not going to Hilltop'?" I turned around to look at Madelyn to see if she was trying to tease me. "Everybody we know who goes away to camp goes to Hilltop."

"That's not the only camp in the world, Amanda."

"I know that. Crestview is a camp, and that's in the world. But black kids don't go to Crestview. Only white kids go there. Black kids go to Hilltop."

"Yes, but there are camps in other places where black kids go. Some where black and white kids even go together." Madelyn got this funny little smile on her face. "Like where you're going."

"Like where? Where am I going to camp, Madelyn? Com'on, you gotta tell me!"

Sometimes my sister can get on my nerves more than anybody I know. This was beginning to be one of those times. I wanted to shake her until she told me what I wanted to know.

Madelyn's little, weird smile stayed on her face like it was glued there. "Look, Amanda," she said, "Mother is looking forward to telling you all of this herself, so just wait for the rest of the details. And pleeeeeease don't let on that you know anything. But trust me. Going to camp is going to be a great experience. You're going to have a great summer."

"Right," I said. "Just great."

From where I was sitting on Madelyn's bed, I could see both of our faces in the mirror. Madelyn's face with the smile that wouldn't go away, and my face that would probably never get a smile again.

Yeah, just great. The greatest worst *summer of my life.*

Week 2

3 ❧ *Ernestine*

"JAZZ, TURN OFF the record player. You can listen to that later."

"Wait, Mama. I want to show you somethin' I learned how to do. Listen."

"Did you hear what I said, Jazz?"

"But—"

"JAZZ!"

"Okay, okay."

It was so much fun watching Jazz dig herself into trouble, I was beginning to forget why Mama had called a family meeting in the living room. That was probably good since I wasn't supposed to know. And I could tell from the way Marcus had looked at me when I came in the living room that he was daring me to *not* be surprised when I heard what Mama and Daddy had to tell us.

Jazz flopped down on the couch between me and Marcus

and folded her skinny arms across each other. I didn't even have to look at her face to know she was pouting. Jazz is a champion pouter and always pouts when things don't go her way.

Daddy was the last one to come in. Even if I hadn't known that we were about to hear bad news, I could have figured it out by looking at my father's long, droopy face. Mama must have been able to tell how he was feeling, too. She perched on the arm of the chair Daddy sat in and put her arm around his shoulders. Then she kinda laid her head against his.

I like seeing my parents together. Even when things are fine and not messed up like Marcus had said they were. Mama and Daddy are always holding hands and doing mushy stuff like that. Sometimes I think they look kinda icky, but watching them always makes me feel good inside. Like seeing how they were in the chair. I started feeling better even without knowing any reasons why I should.

It was raining outside and coming down hard. The globs of rainwater collected in the drain pipes made big splashing sounds when they fell on the ground.

Splup. Splup. Splup.

For a long time the splashing was all I heard. Nobody said anything. Mama kinda looked at Daddy, and Daddy kept looking at his hands and bending and unbending his fingers. Then after what seemed like forever, he cleared his throat, looked at the three of us on the couch, and started talking.

"Kids, there's no easy way to break bad news. I've always contended that the best way is to get on with it. So that's what I'm gonna do—just get on with it."

Daddy started wrapping his fingers up together. Like little kids do when they're playing that here's-the-church, here's-the-steeple game. I think moving his fingers around was making it easier for him to talk to us.

"For the past couple of years, business at Green's has been ...well, it's been terrible. Going downhill the entire time."

Green's is the store where my father works. It's probably called Green's because Mr. Clifford Green owns it. Daddy said it was Mr. Green's father who started the store, but that must have been a long time ago because Mr. Clifford Green the son is an old man.

"Several months ago, Cliff decided to call it quits." Daddy started tapping his two long fingers together. The two sides of the church steeple. "Cliff's first thought was to sell the store."

Daddy stopped tapping and looked at us. "As a matter of fact, for several weeks your uncle J. B. and I tossed around the idea of buying it," he said.

Daddy and Uncle J. B. owning the store? And probably changing the name from Green's to Harris's? I could feel my eyes getting wide.

Daddy pulled his hands apart and broke the steeple. "But after taking many hard looks at the money it would take and how much we had and could borrow, we knew there was no way we could entertain that idea."

My eyes got regular again.

"So it boils down to this simple fact: Green's is closing down, and I'm out of a job."

Daddy's face got even more droopy. I felt mine getting the same way.

"Daddy, Mr. Green says you're his right-hand man. Can't you be his right-hand man for whatever he's gonna do next?"

Jazz's dumb question made Daddy almost smile. For once I was glad she had said something.

"Daddy *was* Cliff's right-hand man, baby," Mama said, smiling at Jazz. "Daddy did everything in that store. He kept the books, ordered inventory, put together ads—"

Daddy cut Mama off. "Com'on now, Lou," he said. He looked at Mama and rubbed one of the steeple fingers across her cheek. "Don't make it sound so special. I was just doin' my job."

In my mind I could see Daddy standing behind the counter in Green's—the way he looked in the light blue coat he always wore while he was working. I could hear him laughing and talking with Miss Sallie who used to come in the store practically every day. "Gracious, Ernest," she would say, "you got i-de-ahs about ever'thin'."

"Daddy," I said, "*any* store would be lucky to have you. How come you just can't work in another store?"

Mama and Daddy looked at each other. Then Daddy said, "The fact is, Ernestine, Green's is, ah, was the only store of any size in Carey owned by a black person. And no white store in town is going to hire a black man to do what I did at Green's—you know, be in charge of things."

Everything got quiet again.

Splup. Splup. Splup.

Then Mama and Daddy looked at each other again, but this time they kinda smiled. Daddy reached for Mama's hand. "But as the saying goes," he said, "it's a truly bad wind that blows not one breath of good."

"Huh?" Jazz and I said the same thing at the same time.

"Good can come out of anything, even from something bad. That's what Dad means," Marcus said. He patted Jazz on the head and winked at me.

"What good can come out of Daddy losing his job?" I asked.

"If you stop talkin' for a minute, maybe you'll find out," Marcus answered, winking again.

Daddy scooched forward in his chair, like he wanted to get closer to us. "After thinking everything over and considering all our options, your mother and I decided to regard this situation as a blessing in disguise."

"Another way to put it," Mama said, "is that instead of feeling like we've lost something, we've decided to act like we've gained something. And what we've gained is an opportunity for your father to start on the road to something he's always wanted to do."

"And we believe that road will give all of us new opportunities," Daddy said.

"What road? Where are we going?" Jazz said, almost yelling.

I expected Mama to tell Jazz to watch it, but all she did was laugh. Daddy did, too.

"Thanks for reminding us, Jazz," Daddy said. "We are being a bit oblique here." He looked at Mama. "Time to lay it on the table, wouldn't you say, sweetheart?"

Mama shook her head to mean "yes," and got up to stand behind Daddy's chair. "Daddy's going to go back to school to work on his Master's degree so he'll be able to teach college courses like he's dreamed of doing," she said. "And that means, *I'll* be the major breadwinner of the family. For a couple of years at least."

"What store will *you* be working in, Mama?" Jazz asked.

"None, baby," Mama said, laughing. "I plan to start teaching full time."

Ever since Jazz started school, Mama has been doing substitute teaching. One time she told me she wanted to teach full time but that she couldn't because she didn't have all of her certification—courses and other stuff the school board said she needed to have to be a full-time teacher.

"Did you get your certification, Mama?" I asked.

I could tell Mama was happy I remembered something she had explained to me a long time ago. "Not yet, sugar," she said, "but I'm going to work on getting it this summer."

Daddy stood up and put his arm around Mama. "So, with the help of our children, these parents are going to become students."

"You mean we can help you with homework and stuff?"

Everybody laughed when Jazz said that, even me. But I still thought it was a dumb thing to ask.

"Not yet, Jazz," Daddy said, "but maybe in a few months. Right now, what we want and need most is your cooperation with the plans we've outlined."

"Marcus," Mama said, reaching out for Marcus's hand, "you've been doing your share of helping out for a while now. All your summer jobs over the past few years and the money you've earned..."

"...and saved, thanks to you and Dad," Marcus said. He got up and kissed Mama on the cheek. "For the record, I think the master plan is pretty cool."

"And thanks to *you*," Daddy said, shaking Marcus's hand, "a lot of the money you'll need for college is already in the bank. That money and your scholarship will help put us over."

It was beginning to get icky, but that was okay. I was mainly glad things weren't so bad as Marcus had said. I started getting up from the couch to get my family hug in.

"And you, Ernestine," Mama said, rubbing my cheek with her hand, "will be helping us by spending a few weeks away at camp."

It was like a bomb dropping on my head. Camp! I had practically wiped it from my brain. Ever since Marcus had told me about Daddy losing his job, I figured the camp thing would go away. After all, camp took money and we needed to save ours. Especially now.

"But, this isn't a good time for me to go to camp. I can help more by staying here. It would save money, and—"

"Ernestine," Mama said. "Listen to me. It will help us a great deal for you to go to camp. It's something Daddy and I want for you very much. Furthermore, we've been putting away money for it all year. A fund especially for you to go to Hilltop."

Daddy put his hands on my shoulders and used his pet name for me. "Buddy," he said, "Mama and I will be able to devote more of our attention to what we have to accomplish if we know that you and Jazz aren't being neglected. That you both have special summer plans."

Jazz started jumping up and down. "Whoopee!" she yelled. "I'm going to camp!"

"Hold on there, baby girl," Daddy said. He lifted Jazz up

in his arms like she was still a little girl. “I didn’t say *you* were going to camp.”

“How come I can’t go to camp like Ernestine?” Jazz said. She was beginning to pout.

“You’ll be visiting Grandmother Carroll in Virginia,” Mama said. “Remember Grandmother’s farm and how you said you wanted to go there?”

“I never said that!” Jazz was almost yelling.

I never said I wanted to go to dumb camp.

I felt like yelling at my parents, too, but I didn’t.

By now all of us were standing together in the middle of the living room. It was still raining hard, and we could still hear the splashing globs of water.

Splup. Splup. Splup.

The family meeting was over and the bad-good news wasn’t a secret any more. Jazz was still pouting, and I knew she would keep on pestering Mama and Daddy about her special summer plans until she was actually at Grandmother Carroll’s. I also knew it was useless for me to say anything else about going to camp. Mama and Daddy had made their decision. I was going and that was that.

My summer is going straight down the drain just like that rain water. Splup. Splup. Splup.

4 ❧ *Amanda*

FRIDAY NIGHT while we were having dinner, Mother and Dad told me about going away to camp. Dad started in his everything's-going-to-be-fine voice. Lately he uses it a lot. "Amanda," he said, "you're in for a treat."

Madelyn looked at me. I knew she was daring me to say anything.

"I can't imagine what," I said. I hoped it would make Madelyn nervous.

"Well, imagine this," he said. "Imagine spending part of the summer in a place with rolling hills to gaze on, a cool lake to swim in, boats to sail in, and horses to ride. How does that sound to you?"

For the first time I wished I hadn't known anything about camp—that Madelyn hadn't told me anything that was going to happen. Then I might have felt happy about what Dad was saying. At least for a little while. Now all I could do was pretend to be happy.

"That sounds good, Dad," I said and pretended to smile.

"What it is, is wonderful," Mother said. She had an everything's-going-to-be-fine voice, too, but hers was weird. Like she didn't believe herself what she was saying.

"Your father and I have found an excellent camp," she said, "and we think that going there for a few weeks will be a wonderful way for you to spend the summer."

Dad smiled like he was glad Mother was happy about it, too. He reached for the rice while Mother kept talking.

"The camp has a marvelous reputation, and the setting is beautiful. We have some brochures upstairs that you can look at after dinner."

I knew that if Mother kept talking she would answer some of my questions without me having to say anything.

"We heard about the camp from the Morrises. Cynthia went there when she was about your age."

I wanted to say, "So what!" But I didn't. Mother thinks the Morrises are great. Cynthia Morris is one of Madelyn's friends, but I don't like Cynthia. To me she's super stuck up. Edna says Cynthia acts like she does because the Morrises have a lot of money. Cynthia's father owns a funeral home, so maybe they are rich. That's still no excuse for acting stuck up.

"It should be quite an experience for you," Mother went on. "In addition to everything else, you'll be going to camp with white children."

Daddy cleared his throat. "Well," he said, "it isn't the presence of white kids that makes the camp any better. It's the fact that—"

"Of course it does," Mother said, interrupting Dad. "Why do you think Camp Castle is as nice a place as it is? It's because—"

This time Dad interrupted, and his voice was a lot louder. "It's as nice as it is because of the economic backing the camp has had for years and continues to have," he said. The left side of Dad's face was beginning to move like it does when he gets mad. "It's economics, Elizabeth. Money, plain and simple. *That's* what defines the difference."

"So you're saying that Camp Hilltop would be your first choice for Amanda," Mother said. She was glaring at Dad.

"If you will recall, my dear, Hilltop *was* my first suggestion when this camp thing was first discussed."

This camp thing?

I looked at Dad out the corner of my eye. The left side of his face was moving like crazy.

"There's *nothing* wrong with Hilltop," he said. "It's a beautiful setting, a lovely camp...if Hilltop had the economic support it deserves from the state, it—"

Mother interrupted again. "It would probably still be an unspectacular place. A camp without flair or appeal. *Nothing* to compare with Camp Castle."

"Listen, Elizabeth—"

"Don't you 'listen, Elizabeth' me, George. I have just as much right to express..."

I couldn't believe what was happening. My parents were arguing about camp. Some stupid, *STUPID* camp! Something nobody but them had brought up in the first place. Just like always, turning everything into a big mess.

Just like always!

I don't remember getting up from the table or anything, but all of a sudden I was standing beside my chair and my plate was laying upside down on the dining-room floor. The rice and meat and gravy that had been on the plate were splattered all over the carpet.

When I looked up, I saw Madelyn staring at me. She had that look on her face—that "chin up, Amanda, everything's gonna be okay" look.

I slapped the table with both of my hands. "It is *not* gonna be okay," I said. I was screaming. "It's *NOT!*"

I ran out of the dining room before anybody could say anything to me. I knew I was going to get into trouble for hitting the table and for raising my voice to my parents, but I didn't care. I just wanted to get away from my messed-up, everything's-going-to-be-terrible family and be by myself.

Going anywhere *will be better than staying in this house, even going to camp! And I don't care what camp it is just as long as it takes me away from here!*

5 Ernestine

"I WOULD SO rather go to Hilltop than to Georgia!"

"Would not!"

"Would, too!"

"Would not!"

"Would, too!"

"Clovis, you tellin' a big fat lie! You would *not* rather go to dumb Hilltop than to see your father, and you know it! You're just sayin' you would, tryin' to make me feel better."

"Ernestine, if you think I'm doin' somethin' to make you feel better, how come you're yellin' at me?"

I looked at Clovis and he looked at me. Then both of us fell out laughing.

I was glad I had come over to Clovis's house. Clovis and I both like to sit on the edge of his grandmother's back porch and listen to the crickets and katydids that Mrs. Taylor, Clovis's grandmother, who he lives with, calls her own private symphony. I like being there because it's so peaceful I can almost forget all the stuff that's going wrong. Like having to go to dumb old Hilltop.

"How come you keep saying 'dumb old Hilltop'?" Clovis asked, looking at me over the top of his glasses.

"Because it *is* dumb. It's way out in the middle of nowhere and—"

"Ernestine, a camp should be way out in the middle of nowhere. Camp should be some place where you can get away from things." Clovis started swinging his legs. His shoes hit against the wood lattice under the porch.

THUMP-thump. THUMP-thump.

"Besides," he said, "It's beautiful up at Hilltop. It's up in the mountains, there're a lot of trees and stuff, and in the summer it stays nice and cool up there even when it's hot everyplace else."

"How come you know so much about Hilltop?"

" 'Cause I went up there last year with Gramma. When she went to Hilltop."

I practically fell off the porch. "Your grandmother went to *camp?*"

Clovis laughed. "No, girl," he said, "the church used Hilltop for a retreat or something. Gramma said a lot of organizations do that, you know, use the camp for special things."

"What else is up there besides trees and stuff?" I asked.

"Camp stuff."

THUMP-thump. THUMP-thump.

"Don't be a pain, Clovis. What's camp stuff?"

"Let's see. There's a big building where most everybody

sleeps and eats." Clovis kinda rocked his head from side to side while he talked. "There're some small buildings, too, but I don't know what they're for."

"Are there just buildings? Isn't there anything for people to do?"

"It's a camp, Ernestine," Clovis said, looking at me over his glasses again. "Of *course* there're things for people to do."

"Like what?" I felt like yelling at Clovis, but I didn't.

"Like swimming. There's a big swimming pool," he said. "And there's a big field people use to play baseball and pitch horseshoes. We pitched horseshoes while we were up there."

THUMP-thump. THUMP-thump.

"Isn't there anything else?"

Clovis stopped swinging his feet. "Look, Ernestine," he said, "when I was at Hilltop, I was with a bunch of people from Gramma's church. They weren't ordinary...you know, campers. I don't know what campers do there, but I *do* know that Hilltop isn't all that bad. *I* don't think it's bad at all."

I started swinging my feet back and forth. Then Clovis started back.

Thump-THUMP-thump. Thump-THUMP-thump.

"Anyhow," Clovis said, "I'd still rather be going to Hilltop like you than to Georgia. *That's* where it's dumb to go in the summer."

Clovis and I listened to the symphony for a long time without saying anything. Then I remembered something I hadn't told him that I knew he'd want to know.

"Guess where I'm going Saturday?" I said. I knew Clovis wouldn't answer, and he didn't. He wants to know everything but hates people to ask him to 'guess' anything.

"Since I know you're about to bust, I'll tell you," I said

after Clovis had stopped swinging his feet and was starting to tap his fingers on the porch.

"I've been invited to Amanda Clay's birthday party."

Clovis's eyes got wide behind his glasses. "Since when have you and Amanda been friends?"

"We aren't. Not really."

I remembered how Amanda and I had practically hated each other at first. I couldn't stand how stuck up she acted most of the time. I'd gotten to know her a little bit because of music lessons at Miss Elder's and the recital. Of course, my brother was going with Amanda's sister, but that was his problem and had nothing to with me being friends with Amanda.

"When I first got the invitation, I thought Amanda's sister Madelyn had asked her to invite me because of Marcus."

I remembered how I said that to Marcus, but he said Amanda wouldn't let her sister help her with anything that had to do with her precious party.

"But now I think Alicia asked Amanda to invite me."

Alicia has been good friends with Amanda since they were little. Alicia and I have become good friends since I started taking music lessons. I figured this gave Amanda a huge pain.

"I bet Amanda's pretending she wants me to come to the party so she can stay on Alicia's good side," I said. "Knowing Amanda, she probably figures she should keep her eye on me and Alicia to make sure our friendship isn't better than hers and Alicia's."

Clovis shook his head in that same way his grandmother does when she's saying "Uh, uh, uh."

"This is gonna be one peculiar summer," I said. "I wish I

could look into a crystal ball to see how it's gonna turn out."

"You know what I wish?" Clovis said. He didn't wait for me to answer. "I wish I could spend the whole summer right here in the back yard. Right over there on Uncle Lemuel's hammock with a whole bunch of books stacked up to read and all the lemonade on earth."

"You'd get really bored," I said.

"Not for a long, long time, I bet."

"Would so."

"Would not."

"Would so."

"Would not."

"Would so."

Week 3

6 Amanda

I COULDN'T BELIEVE it! Ernestine was hanging around Alicia like she was glued to Alicia's arm. Every time I saw Alicia I saw Ernestine. And every time I saw the two of them I wished I had said a big fat "NO!" when Alicia had asked me to invite Ernestine to my party.

When Madelyn said I should go in and bring out more food, I went over to ask Alicia to help. Before I finished my sentence, Ernestine said, "I can help, too." Before I could say we didn't *need* any more help, Alicia had said that would be good.

As soon as we got in the kitchen, Ernestine started looking around at everything. I really didn't care what she thought, but I *was* glad Mother always keeps our kitchen so clean and straight that it looks like a picture in a magazine. Even though we were having my birthday party out in the back yard, there wasn't any mess in the kitchen. The trays of sandwiches and bottles of ginger ale for the punch were lined across the counter. My birthday cake was on a big glass platter and sitting in the middle of the table in the breakfast nook. Mother said putting it there would keep it perfect until we were ready to light the candles. Everything else in the kitchen had been put away.

"Your house is pretty, Amanda," Ernestine said.

I don't think anybody can tell what a house is like just by seeing the kitchen, but I said "thank you" anyway.

Ernestine stood in the doorway of the kitchen and looked into the dining room. "This house seems a lot like yours, Alicia," she said, "or is it my imagination?"

"Nope," Alicia said. "The houses *are* a lot alike. They were designed by the same architect." Alicia grabbed Ernestine's hand. "Can I show her around, Amanda?" Alicia asked.

There wasn't anything I could say. Alicia was already leading Ernestine out of the kitchen. All I could do was follow them.

The Raymonds' house *is* a lot like ours, although I think ours is prettier. Mostly because of the way Mother keeps everything. There's hardly ever anything out of place in our house, and the Raymonds have stuff everywhere. They never have every room straight at the same time, even when they have parties. When I was over there once, Mrs. Raymond started laughing while Alicia and Edna were moving things around to make a place for us to do our homework. "It's called organized chaos, Amanda," she said, "and it'll be fine as long as it doesn't turn into *un*organized chaos."

I don't know exactly what Mrs. Raymond meant, but I

laughed, too. Sometimes when I'm over at the Raymonds' I'm glad things don't have a special place where they always have to be. It's easy to relax over at the Raymonds'....

Alicia had led Ernestine into our living room. "That's the picture I was telling you about," Alicia said, pointing to the photograph on the mantel. "Amanda, tell Ernestine about the picture."

I was getting ready to explain, but Alicia kept on talking. "That's a picture of Amanda's father with Langston Hughes," she said. "They sat next to each other on a train one time, and Mr. Clay said they talked almost the whole entire night while they rode."

Ernestine got closer to the picture. I hoped she wouldn't move it off the mantel. She'd never get it back in the right place.

"Amanda's mother came to the station to meet the train, and she took the picture," Alicia said, keeping on with the story herself. "Mr. Langston Hughes got off the train just for the picture."

I touched the frame without moving it. "Dad got off at a stop the train made before it got to Carey and called mother to ask her to bring a camera when she came to meet the train," I said. "Dad had the picture enlarged because he's so proud of it."

I looked at Ernestine right in the face. "You know who Langston Hughes is, don't you?"

I waited for her to say something smart, but she didn't.

"Mrs. Lawson—she was my fifth-grade teacher," Ernestine said, "she used to read Langston Hughes's poems to us all the time. I even memorized a couple."

"You did?" Alicia said, looking at Ernestine with her eyes all bugged out like Ernestine had done something so wonderful.

"I have a book of poems that Langston Hughes autographed for me and Madelyn," I said. Now *that* was something wonderful.

"She sure does, Ernestine," Alicia said. "Amanda, why don't you show the book to Ernestine?"

"Ernestine probably doesn't want to see some old book," I said. "Anyhow, we have to get back outside."

"Maybe another time," Alicia said.

Not if I can help it.

I led the way back to the kitchen. "Alicia knows just about everything I have," I said. I looked over my shoulder at Ernestine who was following Alicia who was following me. "You know, since we've been best friends almost our whole lives, we know almost everything about each other."

Just so you'll know, Ernestine.

Ernestine didn't say anything. Neither did Alicia, but that was okay. She knew I was telling the truth.

When we got back to the kitchen, Ernestine saw the brochure for Camp Castle Mother had pinned to the little board we have on the wall next to the refrigerator. "Where's this?" she said.

"That's where I'm going to camp," I said.

"Wow," Ernestine said. She said it so soft I almost didn't hear her.

Alicia was looking at the brochure with Ernestine even though she had already seen it. "Ernestine's going to camp, too," she said.

"I'm going to Hilltop," Ernestine said. "I've never been there, but I don't think it's anything like this."

"Camp is camp, I suppose," Alicia said, "no matter where it is."

"Yeah," Ernestine said. "In my opinion, *every* camp is a big pain. And I bet I'll still be saying that exact same thing when I get back home."

Ernestine and Alicia looked at each other like what Ernestine said had a special meaning. I recognized the look. It was one Alicia and I used to give each other a lot.

I reached for one of the plates on the counter. "Everybody says Camp Castle is terrific," I said. "It even has horseback riding." I handed the plate of sandwiches to Alicia.

"It has sailing, too. Cynthia Morris said I should be sure to learn how to sail," I said, handing a bowl of chips to Ernestine.

"You know Cynthia Morris, don't you, Ernestine," I said. I grabbed a bottle of ginger ale and pushed open the screen door. "Her father owns that big funeral home. She used to go to Camp Castle when she was my age."

I held the door open for Alicia and Ernestine so they wouldn't have trouble carrying the things outside. "So, I don't think camp will be a pain at all."

And I bet I'll have a zillion more things to tell Alicia about camp than you will, Fatso Ernestine. Just wait. You'll see.

Week 4

7 Ernestine

"I'M REALLY GOING to miss you, baby," Mama said. She started rubbing her nose against my cheek like she used to do sometimes when she came in to say good night. It made me feel nice but also kinda funny at the same time. Funny because I was sure some of the other kids waiting to get on the bus could see Mama getting kinda icky.

"Aw, Mama," I said, trying not to pull back so I wouldn't hurt her feelings.

Sometimes I *know* Mama can read my thoughts. This turned out to be one of those times.

"Sorry," she said, talking real soft, "I know you're my grown-up girl, and I promise I won't embarrass you. It's just that this is the first time you're going away from home...all by yourself."

I didn't say anything when Mama said that, but I wanted to. *You and Daddy are the ones who want me to go. Not me.*

"Mama, I'm gonna go say good-bye to Jazz," I said. Mama's eyes were getting that watery look, so for once I was glad my peculiar sister was being herself and giving me an excuse to get away for a minute.

Ever since we got to Banneker, where the bus going to Hilltop was parked, Jazz had been sitting by herself in the car. She had refused to get out. When Daddy asked why she had bothered to come since she could have stayed at home with Marcus, she said, "Maybe I'll find somebody at the bus place to adopt me. Then maybe my new parents will send me to camp with *your* daughter, Ernestine."

"Hey, Jazz," I said, climbing into the car. "Find any new parents yet?"

Jazz didn't say anything. She didn't even look at me. She just sat there pouting with her arms folded.

"Com'on, Jazz. Don't be mad at *me*. I'm not the one who said you couldn't go to camp and had to go to Grandmother Carroll's."

Jazz turned around and glared at me. "You oughta be the one goin' to Grandmother's," she said. "You the one named after her, Ernestine *Carroll* Harris. And anyhow it is so your fault that you're going to camp insteadda me."

"How you figure that?"

" 'Cause Mama and Daddy are hopin' camp will help you lose some weight. That's why. So maybe if you hadn't eaten so much they would be sendin' me to camp insteadda you!"

The words had popped out of Jazz's mouth real fast. I could tell by the look on her face that she was sorry as soon as she heard them herself. My sister is more peculiar than anybody I know, but there's one thing she isn't: She's not mean. She wouldn't hurt anybody on purpose, even me.

This time I was the one who sat there not saying anything.

Jazz started pulling on my blouse. "Ernestine, I'm sorry," she said. "You aren't...you're not all that fat and anyhow you know Daddy says it's still baby fat and—"

I cut Jazz off. "Forget it, Jazz," I said. "I know what I...I know how I look. There's only one thing I wanna know. How do *you* know that losing weight is why Mama and Daddy want me to go to camp?"

"I heard them talkin' in the kitchen. Right after the family meeting. All of us went to the kitchen to get some cake, only you left with yours to go out on the back porch. Remember? You said you wanted to listen to the rain."

"Yeah, so?"

"So, Mama saw that great big hunk of cake you cut for yourself and she said somethin' to Daddy about maybe being at Hilltop would help take your mind offa food, and Daddy said he did, too, and that would make the whole sack of ice worth it."

Jazz looked at me for the first time since she had started talking. "Ernestine, why was Daddy talkin' about a sack of ice?"

I started laughing. I couldn't help myself. "Jazz," I said, and reached over to give my peculiar little sister a hug, "Daddy said 'sacrifice.' He meant...oh, never mind. He didn't mean anything important."

I figured Jazz would start bugging me to tell her anyway, but she didn't. Both of us just sat there being quiet, one of us wishing that she wasn't going to camp and the other one wishing she was.

Two sisters. Both of them peculiar.

When the bus pulled off, everybody was leaning out the windows, waving and saying good-bye. I was, too, even though at first I didn't want to. I thought looking at Mama and Daddy and Jazz standing there, waving and throwing me kisses, would make me cry. It didn't, though.

It was going to be a long ride to Hilltop—Daddy had said about two hours. Even though all the girls on the bus were from Carey, where we lived, I didn't see anybody I knew. Some of the girls knew each other and were sitting together and talking. But there wasn't anybody in the seat next to me.

I was glad Mama had suggested I put one of my books in the overnight case I was going to keep with me. I had packed a bunch of other books in the big suitcase. "I hope you don't try to read all those books," Mama had said when she saw my stack of books. "If you read your time away, you'll miss the joys of camp."

After hearing what Jazz had told me, I figured I knew now what Mama really meant.

She's afraid I'll miss the joys of exercise.

I was fishing around in the case when somebody tapped me on the shoulder. I turned around and looked into the face of the girl in the seat behind me. I had seen her when everybody was getting on the bus.

"Hi," she said.

"Hi," I said back.

"I saw you with your parents," she said. "Was the little girl your sister?"

"Um-hm. Her name is Jess—, ah Jazz."

"I wish I had a sister. I only have brothers. Three brothers."

I was getting ready to say she should be glad she didn't have a sister, especially one who was peculiar and a pest most of the time. But it didn't feel right to say that about Jazz to someone who didn't know her.

"My name is Ernestine," I said. "What's yours?"

"Deena," she said. "Deena Lewis."

Deena smiled at me and I smiled back. "Hi, Deena," I said.

"Ernestine, do you mind if I move up there and sit next to you?"

"That'll be great," I said. I closed the top of the overnight case.

At first I thought I wouldn't know what to talk about, but Deena talked enough for both of us. She told me about her family and her best friend, Brenda.

"Brenda wanted to come to camp real bad, but her parents are very strict. They won't let Brenda go anyplace where they can't know what's going on every single minute."

She told me about her school, which I had heard of because Mama substitutes there sometimes, and about her dog, Him Howard Too.

I laughed when she told me the dog's name. "That's a peculiar name for a dog," I said.

Deena agreed. "Yeah, it is. When we first got the dog, my baby brother, whose name is Howard, also, would point to the dog and say, 'him Howard, too.' My parents thought it was so cute *they* started calling the dog that. I tried calling the dog Nutmeg—that's what I wanted to name him because that's the color he is—but nobody else would call him that. After a while the only thing the dog would answer to was Him Howard Too."

Deena explained why she thought the "Too" of the dog's name should be spelled T-w-o since he was the second Howard in the family. Then she told me about some of the other names people have in her family. She went on and on and on. About her Girl Scout troop, about her favorite movies, about everything!

That Deena sure can talk!

The bus was climbing the road up into the mountains. That mountain air blowing through the open windows was cool and fresh. It smelled nice—like new air. The problem was that all that new air and Deena's voice were like a lullaby, making me so sleepy I could hardly keep my eyes open.

I tried and tried to stay awake. I rested my head on the arm I had propped up on the back of the seat. That way I could use my arm to hold one of my eyes open while I listened. When that didn't work, I exercised my tongue against my teeth while I listened. After Deena looked at my face and asked me a couple of times if anything was wrong, I stopped. Then, I just gave up.

"Deena," I said. "I'm getting sleepy. It's the bus, I think. I always get sleepy riding on a school bus."

It's only a little fib and it won't hurt anybody.

"Me, too," Deena said. "I get sleepy riding in anything, even trains. There was that time..."

I think Deena kept talking, but I don't know for sure because that's when I fell asleep.

The next thing I remember was Deena shaking my shoulder. "Ernestine," she said. "Ernestine, wake up. We're here."

The bus was moving on a long driveway, making big crunching noises. The driveway was made of gravel. Other yellow school buses like ours were parked along the driveway, all of them pointed in the direction of the big building that was straight ahead. I figured there were other buildings somewhere, but it was hard to see them. The only thing I could see for sure were trees. Everywhere. A million of them.

Deena leaned over so she could look out the window, too. "I think that's where campers sleep," she said, pointing to the long building.

"Ernestine," she said, looking at me, "we can share a bunk! That would be good, don't you think?"

Before I could say anything, the woman who had checked off our names when we got on the bus stood up. She said, "Campers, welcome to Hilltop! The camp at the top of the mountain!"

All of a sudden, pictures in the little book I had seen in Amanda's kitchen popped in my head. The pictures showed a camp building that looked kinda like a castle and a big sparkly lake with sailboats on it. One picture even had kids riding horses through a field with lots of grass.

And here I am at a camp at the top of a dumb old mountain, surrounded by trees and probably bears and snakes. Maybe even mountain lions!

"Yeah, Deena," I said, "that'll be real good." I started exercising my tongue again. Only this time I did it to keep from crying.

8 Amanda

JUST WAIT UNTIL *Alicia hears about this!*

When we got to the entrance to Camp Castle, I couldn't believe what I saw. It was a real castle! The kind you read about in fairy tales and see in movies. It had a drawbridge and a tower and everything! There was even a moat—but that was mostly a creek that ran under the drawbridge.

"Does the drawbridge really work?" I asked. "I mean, can it be raised up and lowered down again?"

"Sure can. In fact it's raised every night at midnight and lowered again at seven every morning."

I was talking to Derek. He drove the Camp Castle bus that had been waiting at the station when our train came in. The train my godmother, Frankie, and I had been on.

I had been super glad Godmother Frankie was the one bringing me to camp. At first Mother was, but since Godmother Frankie was going to be in summer school in Philadelphia the same time I would be at camp, Dad said it would be a better idea for the two of us to travel to Pennsylvania together. Mother didn't seem to like the idea too much, but she said "okay" anyway.

Riding on the train with my godmother was a terrific way to start my camp adventure. That's what Godmother kept saying about going to camp. "I went off on my first camp adventure when I was eleven," she had said while we were riding along and watching the scenery. "And now my favorite godchild is off on her own camp adventure."

"I'm your *only* godchild, Godmother Frankie," I said.

"That makes it even better," she said. "Nothing could be more special than being the one and only and *still* the favorite!"

I love being with my godmother. She's more fun to be with than any grown person I know. And it's easy to talk with her about almost everything. Everything except the separation. I didn't want to talk to *anybody* about that. But I knew that if I did want to talk about it, I could talk to her. I can trust Godmother Frankie to keep all my secrets. I used to think Madelyn could keep them, too, but now I know she can't. She told Mother a secret she swore she would keep. I think she might have done it because she thought Mother really needed to know, but no matter what, Madelyn told *my* secret without *my* permission. And Mother doesn't keep my secrets. She thinks kids don't even have a right to have them.

My godmother and mother are nothing alike. Sometimes I don't think they even like each other all that much. They never go places together or sit and talk like Godmother does with Dad. Maybe that's because she and Dad have been friends their whole lives—since they were kids and grew up in Louisiana together.

While we were on the train, Godmother talked about things she and my dad used to do when they were growing up—some of the fun they had, but some of the trouble they got into, too. All while she talked I was thinking how glad I was Godmother Frankie would be nearby while I was at camp. It's not that I was afraid or nervous about going to Camp Castle or anything like that. It was just good to know that somebody I knew and could talk to would be close by.

That's what made it easier to say good-bye at the train station. Derek had put my bags on the green bus that had CAMP CASTLE written on it in big white letters. He was wearing a green T-shirt with the same writing on it and had brought one for me to wear if I wanted to. I didn't, but I kept it anyway. Then Derek said he would wait for me on the bus and that I should take my time because I would be the only passenger he had on this run.

Godmother was looking at me, smiling. I couldn't tell how she was really feeling because she had her sunglasses on and I couldn't see her eyes.

"Well, here we are," I said. It sounded weird to say something we both knew, but I couldn't think of anything else.

"Yep, we're here, all right," she said, "and soon to be there."

She pulled her sunglasses down to the end of her nose. It felt good to see her eyes. "And wherever you are, I'll be close by. Know what I mean, jellybean?"

It felt good to smile, too.

I hugged my godmother. "Just remember, baby," she whispered in my ear, "make the best of every new experience and enjoy the camp adventure." Then she kissed me. After I got on the bus. I waved to her and she waved back until I couldn't see her any more.

I think I might have felt terrible if Derek hadn't started talking right away like he did. As soon as we pulled off, he asked if this was my first time at Camp Castle. When I said "yes," he started telling me about it. About it being a castle with stables and an archery field and being near a big lake. I couldn't believe how much he bragged about the place. He sounded like he owned it.

After we crossed over the drawbridge and got to the entrance, Derek pointed to a raised iron gate we were passing under. "That gate works, too," he said. "We call it a 'portcullis.' "

When we got inside, I saw that the castle walls didn't surround the whole camp even though it had looked like they did from the outside. Instead, they curved around on both sides and then stopped. The open part had grass and patches of trees and little paths leading to different places. And everywhere, including on each side of the stopped walls, were sets of little stone houses.

"That's where campers stay," Derek said, pointing to one of the little gray houses. He was parking the bus in a space near the tower. "We call them castle homes. You'll be staying in one."

"Does anybody stay in the tower?" I asked. I imagined the tower having a lot of stories with a curvy staircase leading to each one. "I bet living there would be like living inside a real castle."

Derek laughed. "I bet you wouldn't think that if you lived there," he said. "Camp workers live in the tower. We call it the 'keep.' The wake-up bell in the keep rings at five o'clock so we can get things going—like breakfast."

"What do you call breakfast?"

Derek laughed like I had told a joke or something. I wasn't trying to be funny. So far everything he had told me about had a special name, so I thought meals must have, too.

"Over there's the stable," Derek said, pointing to it. "Sometimes we call that a barn."

When Derek laughed that time, so did I.

In the distance I could see the lake. It was blue like the sky on a perfect day. It was beautiful. The lake and everything else I had seen made it seem like the Camp Castle brochure had come to life. Only better. Now all the separate pictures fit together.

Derek pushed the rod that opened the door of the bus. Finally. I could hardly wait to get off the bus and see what else was part of the castle.

Derek asked me to wait by the bus until he brought out my bags. While I stood there and looked around, I saw some of the other campers. All of them were girls, since Camp Castle is for girls only. Some of them were wearing green T-shirts just like Derek's. Some of them looked like they were about my age; some looked younger and some looked older.

There was a group of girls standing near the door of the tower. Seeing them reminded me of another picture from the brochure. The picture showed girls of different ages standing together near a big curved door just like the tower door. The girls were smiling and looking like they were at the best place in the world.

It was another picture from the brochure that had come to life. In the brochure all the girls were white. Just like all the girls I saw in the group. Just like everybody else I had seen so far at Camp Castle. Even Derek, who was carrying my bags and telling me to follow him. Everybody!

Godmother was right. This is gonna be an adventure, all right. A real camp adventure.

Week 5

9 *Ernestine*

"*RRRRRRREMEMBER*, ladies, here at Hilltop, ours is a *prrrroooud* tradition. This camp has been a mountain summer home to young people of *Afrrrrican* heritage for several *generrrrations*!"

When I looked at Deena and saw her looking at me, I knew she wanted to bust out laughing just like I did. Mrs. Williamson was rolling so many *r*'s, it was getting harder and harder to keep a straight face. I started biting the insides of my cheeks to keep a laugh from popping out.

"Life at Hilltop will *enrrrrrich* your body and your spirit. I urge each of you to make the *verrrrry* best of each and *everrrry* day!"

Deena poked me with her elbow, but I didn't look at her. I knew if I did I might lose it.

"Begin *rrrright* here and now. Use this evening in Tubman Hall to become better acquainted. I, as your leader, will seek *you* out. You must in turn seek each other out. *Grrrrreet* someone new, someone not in your bunk group or at your meal table. Welcome each other into our *prrrroooud* tradition!"

I was so glad everybody started clapping and I could let my laugh out. Whew, what a relief!

"Com'on," Deena said, getting up. All of us had been sitting cross-legged on the floor of Tubman Hall while Mrs. Williamson gave her rolling speech. "Let's go greet somebody new, like she said."

Deena and I had been hanging out together ever since that first day on the bus. We didn't share a bunk like we had planned to, but our bunk rooms were next to each other. All the bunk rooms are on the second floor of the main building, and every camper except junior counselors stay there. Lucky junior counselors get to live in bungalows near the softball field.

I was glad I had made a friend that first day. Hilltop wasn't anywhere near as bad as I had thought it was going to be, but it might have been if I hadn't had anybody to talk to or be with during free times. Like after dinner when everybody gathered in Tubman Hall.

Deena was nice, too. And fun. There was only one problem: sometimes she talked so much that I thought she might talk my ears off. *That* could be a real pain.

Deena was pulling my arm. "Ernestine, let's go over there and greet them," she said, pointing to the girls standing by the door.

"We can't just go over there and...and break in on *them*, Deena," I said.

"Why not?"

"Because."

"Because what?"

"You gotta know what, Deena."

Deena was pointing to a group of junior counselors who were standing and talking together. But they weren't just any junior counselors—both Raelynn Jefferson and Neidra Johnson were in the group. Everybody in the whole camp wanted to be friends with Raelynn and Neidra. They were...they had everything!

I moved closer to Deena so I could explain without anybody else hearing me.

"Raelynn and Neidra and all that bunch of junior counselors don't want to be bothered with some junior *campers*."

Especially one that's too fat.

Deena put her hands on her hips. "How do you know?" she said. "Have you ever talked to either of them? Francene Diggs—she has the bunk next to mine. Francene says Neidra and Raelynn are both real nice, especially Raelynn. She, Francene not Raelynn, was telling us how Raelynn got her name. Her father's name is Raymond and her mother's name is Linda. They named her Raelynn so she could have part of both their names! Isn't that cute? Francene knows because she comes from Logan and that's where Raelynn and Neidra live. You know the two of them are best friends...."

How does she remember all this stuff?

"Okay, okay," I said. "Let's go over and say 'hi.' But then we're gonna keep going and meet some other people, too, okay?"

I figured the only way to shut Deena up would be to just

get it over with. But I still felt kinda dumb walking over to that group.

I had seen Raelynn lots of times but I had never been close to her. I think most people noticed her because of her hair and her walk. Her hair was so long she could practically sit on it, and the way she walked...it was so cool. She moved her hips and shoulders at the same time and kinda used her arm like she was pushing the air away. Whatever it was she was doing, the walk fit her just right. But even without the hair and the walk, Raelynn was very, very cute. And so was her best friend, Neidra. Both of them looked good in cut-off T-shirts that showed their stomachs.

I'd give anything to be able to wear a cut-off T-shirt, but that will probably never happen in my whole entire life.

Raelynn and Neidra were talking to each other when we walked up, but that didn't stop Deena. She jumped right in. "Hi, Raelynn. Hi, Neidra," she said. "My name is Deena and this is Ernestine. We both come from Carey, but we didn't know each other until we got on the bus to come to Hilltop. That's how we met."

She doesn't even KNOW these people. Oh, Deena.

I began to wish I could just dissolve into the air. I didn't want to look at Raelynn or any of the others, but I couldn't stop myself. Then I wished I hadn't. Raelynn had this big grin on her face.

She thinks Deena's a dummy. She KNOWS I'm one because I'm just standing here letting Deena go on and on and on.

I had to try something. "Ah, I—"

I didn't have to decide what else to say. Raelynn interrupted me.

"Did you say you were from Carey?" she asked.

"Yeah," Deena said before I could even shake my head. "Both of us."

"My aunt lives in Carey," Raelynn said. "Her name is Clarice Elder. She teaches music."

Sweet Miss Elder is Raelynn's aunt! It figures.

Deena started again before I could get a word out. "Miss Elder! Actually, I don't know her, but I know who she is. Ernestine takes music lessons from her."

Deena looked at me with this big grin on her face. "Don't you, Ernestine?"

There was nothing left for me to say. All I did was nod my head.

"Ernestine, were you in the recital Aunt Clarice had last spring? The one that featured Camille Nickerson?"

I think I half expected Deena to answer the question for me and that's why I didn't say anything right away. But for once, Deena just stood there with a *closed* mouth.

"Yeah...ah, yes. I was a part of the recital. I—"

Raelynn interrupted me again. "I *knew* I had seen you somewhere before!" She turned to look at Neidra. "See, Neidra, I told you!"

Raelynn put her hand on my arm. "Excuse me for interrupting you, Ernestine, but I told Neidra I recognized you. I just couldn't remember from where."

"Were you at the recital?" I asked.

"My whole family was," Raelynn said, "but we got there late. We had a flat tire driving up from Logan. We sat in the very back of the auditorium and left right away to meet Aunt Clarice at her house."

No wonder. Edna would've been telling everybody about all that long hair.

"So, you do play the piano, right, Ernestine?"

Deena jumped in before I could answer. "She sure does," she said. I guess she could stay quiet only so long.

"Deeeena!" I was feeling embarrassed.

"You know you do, Ernestine," Deena said. "Stop being shy."

"That's right, Ernestine," Neidra said. "Stop being shy and help out the cause. The one thing Hilltop is in dire need of every summer is a good piano player."

She grabbed one of my hands and Raelynn grabbed the other. The two of them led me over to the piano by the window.

"Do you know 'Tell Me Why'?" Neidra asked after they had plunked me down on the piano bench.

"I might," I said. "If you start singing it, I can probably follow along."

Raelynn put her hands in front of her mouth like she was talking through a megaphone. "And what's more, ladies and gentlemen, she plays by ear!" she said. I could tell she wasn't trying to tease me.

Both Raelynn and Neidra started singing.

Tell me why the stars do shine,

I recognized the song. It's one the youth group at my church sings sometimes at the end of a meeting.

Tell me why the ivy twines,

By the third line, I had joined in with some chords that harmonized with the melody.

Tell me why the sky's so blue,

By the end of the first verse some more girls had come up to the piano and were singing along.

And I will tell you some ways God loves you.

Deena was leaning on the top of the piano. She was singing along, too, but her eyes were still talking. To me.

"See, I told you they were nice!" her eyes said, loud and clear.

10 *Amanda*

THE FIRST WEEK at Camp Castle was weird. *Really* weird. In the first place, there were so many things to get used to. Like eating and sleeping with people I had never even *seen* before. And remembering all the camp rules. There were a zillion! But the weirdest of all was learning how things ...well, just how things were.

In Carey where I live, black people and white people hardly do anything together. White people live in different parts of town and white kids go to different schools than we do. Some of the places white people have, black people can't even go to. Like Marvelous Park over near the Dairy Queen. Most of it is just a park with regular park things like benches and water fountains. You can see those parts when you walk by. But in a part of Marvelous Park you can't see from the street is a swimming pool. Dad says the swimming pool is the reason it's a for-white-people-only park. A segregated park.

The movie theaters in Carey are segregated, too. White people can sit anywhere they want, but black people can sit only in the balcony. Dad never goes to the movies and says he never will until he has the right to sit anywhere he pleases. Madelyn and I used to go together, but ever since she started dating Marcus she stopped going to the movies, too. She didn't even go to see *Blackboard Jungle*, and that had a black man starring in it.

I went to see *Blackboard Jungle* with my mother. She says it's silly to deprive yourself of something you have no control over and that the best seats in the theater are in the balcony in the first place. Going to the movies was one of the things my parents used to fuss about.

Things at Castle were very different from home. At Castle, black and white kids did everything together, including swimming. In the movies they had on Friday night, anybody could sit anywhere, except in the very last row, which was reserved for senior counselors. None of us wanted to sit there anyway.

I wasn't the only black girl in the camp like I was afraid I might be when I got off the bus that first day and looked around, but I was the only one in my castle home. (Every castle home was just one big room with beds and dressers and a bathroom.) Except for Marietta Jarvis, nobody in my castle home treated me any different from anybody else. Marietta was stuck up with everybody, but super stuck up with me. Candy, who had the bed next to mine, said that Marietta acted like she did because she grew up in Alabama. Candy knows about things like that since she's lived in different places all over the world. Her father's a colonel in the army, so her family has moved a lot.

Marietta liked to hang around with Patricia Wilshure, one of the richest girls in camp. Her father owns department stores! Patricia even brought her own horse to ride while she was at Castle. But as rich as she is, Patricia treated everybody the same, including Glory, the black girl who lived in Patricia's castle home.

I met Glory my first day at Castle. She was in the great hall where everybody came to register and find out which castle home they would be staying in. She was laughing and talking with some other girls when the senior counselor registering me called her over.

"Glory," the counselor said, "I want you to meet Amanda Clay. The two of you should get to know each other."

I wondered why the counselor thought Glory and I should get to know each other. How did she know we would like the same things? Weird.

Glory said "hi" when the counselor introduced us, but she didn't seem extra friendly. I said "hi" back and didn't say anything else, either.

"This is Glory's second year at Castle," the counselor said. "Glory, maybe you can show Amanda around later."

Glory smiled and said "sure," but she said it more to the counselor than to me. Then she sort of waved at me with her fingers and went back to the group of girls she had been with. All the girls in the group were white.

I think she said something about me when she went back because after she started talking, one of the girls turned around to look at me. Then all of them laughed.

So much for you, Glory.

Another girl I met that first day at registration was Leslie. She reminded me so much of Alicia that sometimes being with her almost made me homesick. She had that same way that Alicia has that makes everybody like her.

Leslie had been to Castle before, too, so she showed me around a little bit that first day. I told her I wished we would have been assigned to the same castle home. She said we'd probably be assigned to the same round table in the great hall because we had the same home counselor. It turned out that Leslie was right; most of the time we sat together for meals.

Leslie was in the same castle home as Charity Peabody. Charity had been coming to Castle for years. She would tell anybody how she knew "all the ropes." She also acted like none of the camp rules made any difference to her. Charity Peabody was something else!

One of the big rules at Castle is being on time for meals. At every mealtime, each girl is supposed to stand behind her chair until a senior counselor sounds the gong, then everybody sits down together. Every chair is supposed to be filled, and the only people standing should be the people serving. Home counselors, who sit at the table with campers they're responsible for, have to report absences right away.

One evening at supper time Charity wasn't behind her chair and hadn't come in by the time the gong sounded. After we all sat down, Kristen, our home counselor, stood up and looked around the whole hall for Charity. She asked if anybody had seen her, but nobody said anything. Then Kristen left the table to report Charity.

The minute Kristen was gone, Charity appeared. She

crawled out from under the table and sorta slid up into her chair! She told us that she had been hiding under there for almost an hour before supper was supposed to begin. That's why nobody had seen her. Then she said to please pass the food so she could start eating.

Kristen almost fell over when she came back and saw Charity sitting at the table. "Charity?" she said, sounding like she couldn't believe what she was seeing. "Where have you been?"

"What do you mean, Kristen?" Charity said. Her eyes were wide like she couldn't believe what Kristen was saying to her. "I've been right here in the dining room. Ever since *before* dinner started."

"Charity, that's a boldface lie!" Kristen said. She was very close to yelling at Charity.

Charity looked Kristen right in the face. "You're calling me a liar?" she asked. Then she looked at some of the others at the table. "Did you hear? Kristen called me a liar."

Charity looked at Kelly McGrath. Kelly already had a reputation as a big mouth. "Kelly," she said, "haven't I been here the whole time? Tell the truth, Kell."

All of us were looking at Charity's face. It was easy to see from her eyes that nobody would even *think* about saying that she hadn't been there. And it *was* sort of the truth.

Kelly looked at Kristen. "Charity's been here the whole time," she said.

"And if you don't stop calling me a liar, Kristen," Charity said, "I might have to report *you*."

Kristen's eyes got narrow and the holes of her nose started going in and out. But she didn't say anything else to Charity.

"Excuse me, kids" she said. "I'm going to the senior counselors' table to change my report. I'll be right back."

After Kristen left, Charity started laughing. Then everybody else at the table started laughing with her.

Leslie leaned over and whispered in my ear. "Charity's something else, isn't she!"

Charity Peabody wasn't like anybody I had ever met before. She was *really* something. She probably never let anything get her down or make her feel bad.

You're one person I'm gonna get to know better, Charity Peabody. Just wait. You'll see.

Week 6

11 Ernestine

"OKAY, AMPERS, hen the histl owes, evody in!"

I unbuckled my swimming cap and pulled back the flaps covering my ears. "What did she say?" I asked the girl standing next to me at the edge of the pool.

Right then the counselor blew her whistle. Everybody jumped into the pool, including the girl I was talking to.

"Harris!" the counselor yelled, and blew her giant whistle.

"Yes?" I said as loud as I could without screaming.

"Anything wrong with your hearing?"

Only that I have to listen to you!

"No, Ma'm," I said. Even though the wind was blowing and it was cool there by the pool, I felt my face getting hot. "I didn't hear what you said."

"I SAID, when the whistle blows, everybody IN! That means you, too, Harris!" Then she blew her monster whistle again.

I tried to jump in the pool like everybody else had done.

Feet first and straight down. But when I told myself "Go," I ended up falling forward and landing on the water flat on my stomach. Water splashed everywhere!

When my feet found the bottom of the pool and I was able to stand up, I heard the others in the pool laughing. I felt so bad I couldn't even blame them. If I had seen somebody plunk into the pool like I did, I'd probably laugh, too.

"HARRIS!"

Miss Rutherford's yell scared me practically to death. My feet slipped and I began to fall backward in the water. I pushed my arms and hands around every way I could, trying to find something in the water to hold onto.

Oh no oh no oh no oh no. I'm gonna fall over in the water again like a whale!

I struggled hard to keep my feet on the bottom, but they wouldn't stay there. It felt like I was getting ready to drown.

At least if I drown, I'll never have to go swimming again.

I was ready to give up when I felt two hands—one on my back and one on my arm. "Steady, Ernestine. Take your time and stand up. You can do it."

The voice belonging to the hands was quiet. It sounded familiar but I knew it didn't belong to Miss Rutherford; her voice was always loud. And most of the time it was evil sounding. It was to me, anyhow.

The hands made it easy for me to stand up. I leaned forward a little so I wouldn't start to fall backward again.

"You okay now?" the voice said.

"I'm okay," I said, blowing water out of my mouth.

"Ernestine's fine, Miss Rutherford," the voice called out. "I'll be her partner."

I had gotten so much chlorine in my eyes that it was hard

to open them. When I did, I saw who belonged to the hands that had saved my life. Raelynn Jefferson.

Standing there beside me in the pool, Raelynn didn't have on a swimming cap like most of us did. Her hair was pulled back in one long braid. She never worried about getting her hair wet. Most of the time after swimming, Raelynn would sit out in front of her bungalow and dry her hair in the sun.

My hair was one of the reasons I hated swimming. Ever since the first time I had gone into the pool, my hair had been a mess. There was no hope for it, and I knew there wouldn't be until I got back home and went to the hairdresser to get it fixed.

But the biggest reason I hated swimming was Miss Rutherford. She was the senior counselor in charge of swimming. From the way she yelled at everybody and called them by their last name, I didn't think Miss Rutherford liked campers, period. And I *knew* I didn't like her.

Miss Rutherford was yelling again. "Okay, Jefferson," she was saying to Raelynn. "Harris is all yours."

Raelynn was standing in front of me, facing me in the water. "Okay, Ernestine," she said. "The first thing we have to do is help you get over your fear of water."

"I don't know how to swim, but I'm not afraid of the water." The words just popped out. I hoped Raelynn didn't think I was being a smart mouth. I didn't want to make her sorry she had bothered to save my life.

"I mean, the water's not the reason I'm so terrible," I said. "It's Miss Rutherford. She yells so much, she makes me scared of practically everything about swimming."

Raelynn laughed. For a minute it felt like I was hearing Alicia. "Ruthie's not so bad," she said.

"You call her *Ruthie?*" My feet slipped again and I began falling backward. Raelynn caught my hand.

"Whoa," she said, helping me get steady again. "Ruthie has really put the fear of the bear in you, hasn't she."

Raelynn took one of my hands in each of hers. It was like kids do when they're getting ready to twirl each other around when they play "Listen to the Rhythm."

"Everybody calls her 'Ruthie,'" she said, "only not to her face. I think she knows we do, though."

"I bet she'd yell like a crazy person if she heard anybody call her Ruthie."

"Probably," Raelynn said, "but, you really shouldn't be scared of her."

Raelynn started walking in a circle. Since she was holding my hands, I had to walk in a circle, too. Right there in the water. It really *was* like we were going to play "Listen to the Rhythm," but I knew we weren't.

"There's something you should remember whenever you hear Ruthie yelling," Raelynn said, still moving in her circle. "Where she grew up she was always hearing about black kids drowning, mainly because they didn't know how to swim. She said she promised herself that one day she would do whatever she could to change those statistics."

Hmmmm. Come to think of it, the only person I know who goes swimming is Alicia. She learned in the ocean.

"How come so many kids didn't know how to swim?" I asked.

Raelynn didn't stop moving, but she looked at me with

one of those "you-got-to-be-kidding" looks. "You're from Carey, right?" she asked.

"Yeah?"

"And where in Carey can *you* go swimming?"

"Nowhere," I said. "There's a swimming pool in Marvelous Park, but we...ah, black kids can't go there."

"Right," Raelynn said. "That's Ruthie's point. In most places where black folks live, there's no place kids can go to swim. That's especially true in Mississippi where she grew up."

Raelynn stopped moving in her circle. I could tell from the way she looked at me that she knew I understood even though I hadn't said anything. "So," she said, "ready to tackle this swimming thing?"

"Ready."

"Okay, then. Let's boogie!"

Raelynn started moving in her circle again. Only this time she moved fast and bounced up and down while she moved. I was able to keep up with her without falling or feeling afraid.

Before it was time to get out of the pool, I had learned how to do several things, including float. Every time I turned over to float on my back, I could feel the cool pool water creeping under my swim cap and into my hair.

My hair's gonna be a mess forever and smell like chlorine longer than that!

Even so, for the very first time since camp had started, I didn't hate being in the swimming pool. Raelynn was making it easy—and fun. And she acted like she didn't mind spending time with me at all. It even seemed like she was having fun the same as me.

Before I got out of the pool, I promised myself that I wasn't going to let Raelynn down. I was going make sure she knew what a great teacher she was.

I'm gonna learn how to swim even if it drowns me. Even if Ruthie keeps yelling HARRIS until her head falls off!

12 ❧ *Amanda*

I STARTED WATCHING for Godmother Frankie right after castle home inspection. I had been so glad she was coming for Visitor's Day. She said she was bringing goodies with her, including my favorite: coconut-lemon cake. I couldn't wait to see her—*and* to have all my friends get to see her.

Godmother Frankie is the sharpest dresser I've ever seen, except for people in movies and Mother's fashion magazines. Godmother always has on something unusual, and everything she wears looks good on her. Mother says clothes hang well on her because Godmother is tall and skinny. She *is* tall, but I don't think she's skinny; she's just not fat *any*-where.

When she came on Visitor's Day, Godmother wore slacks and a sweater. Both were the color of lemons *and* they matched the car she was driving—it was a convertible! (She told me the car belonged to the man she was dating in

Philadelphia.) I almost fainted when she got out of the car and waved to me. She looked *sooooo* good!

Godmother laughed when I told her she looked splashing. "I sure hope that means 'good,' Godchild," she said.

"Absolutely, Godmother. We use it all the time," I told her.

" 'We?' Who's 'we'?"

"My friends here at Castle. Patricia Wilshure uses it so much, the rest of us can't keep from sayin' it too. Patricia's one of the people I want you to meet while you're here."

I couldn't wait to introduce my godmother to my friends, especially Charity.

Charity was more fun to be with than anybody I had ever met. She was always dreaming up wild stuff to do. Like what she did in the senior counselors' bathroom.

One night after lights out, Charity sneaked into the tower—that's where all the senior counselors lived. She went in their bathroom and wrapped every single toilet! Before I came to Castle I didn't know what wrapping a toilet was. It means putting plastic wrap between the toilet seat and the toilet bowl. When somebody gets ready to use the toilet, they can't see the plastic or feel it either, so they go ahead and start using the toilet. But nothing can go down into the toilet bowl because of the plastic wrap. So then...well, what happens then is wild!

After Charity wrapped all the toilets, she sneaked back into her castle home and woke everybody up to tell them what she had done. That's how I found out; my friend Leslie who lived there, too, told me.

The next morning at breakfast Miss Pritchard, the head senior counselor, gave a lecture about respecting the privacy of others. She didn't mention anything in particular and she didn't call anybody's name, but everyone knew she was mad about something.

"Crude pranks have no place in polite society," she said.

Charity started frowning like she couldn't even imagine why Miss Pritchard seemed upset and was giving us a lecture. "Crude pranks? What on earth could Pritchie be talking about?"

Everybody at our round table started giggling, everybody except Kristen who hates anything Charity says.

Later, on the way to the lake for swimming, I saw Charity walking ahead of me and ran to catch up with her. I told her how splashing I thought her "crude prank" was.

"Did you see how pinched up Pritchie looked this morning?" Charity started imitating Miss Pritchard's voice. "'Here at Castle we don't try to gain satisfaction for ourselves at the expense of others,'" she said, turning up her nose like Miss Pritchard does.

"I would have been plenty satisfied if I could've seen Pritchie Poo sitting down on one of those toilets this morning," Charity said, laughing like crazy.

We kept walking along together. "Now if I could just think of some way to get out of swimming," Charity said.

"You don't like swimming, either?" I was surprised to hear Charity say she hated swimming. She was a terrific swimmer. I hated it because I didn't know how.

"Swimming's a yawn," Charity said. "I go swimming all the time, especially in the winter when I visit my father in Florida."

Visit your father in Florida? What about your mother?

I wanted to ask Charity about her parents, but didn't know if I should or not.

"It's a yawn for me, too," I said, "but I can't swim anywhere near as good as you."

Actually I can't swim at all.

"I'll teach you," Charity said. Just like that. Without me even asking her to or anything. And that's what she did every day at the lake when it was time for swimming. She was *sooooo* much fun. My friend, Charity Peabody!

When I was on my way to my castle home with the box of food Godmother Frankie had brought me, I ran into Charity.

"Charity, where've you been?" I asked. "We looked for you everywhere. I wanted you to meet my Godmother Frankie."

"Visitor's Day is a complete yawn," Charity said. "I've been out sailing."

"You *have*? I thought the sailboats were off limits today."

Charity looked at me like I had said something stupid. "They were," she said. "So?"

I should have known by then that there wasn't anything Charity wasn't brave enough to do. Even take out a sailboat by herself on Visitor's Day. Since she was acting like it was no big deal, I did, too.

"So, nothing," I said, shrugging my shoulders like she had. "I'm just sorry my godmother didn't get to meet you."

"What's in the box?"

"Food my godmother brought me. I'm taking it home," I said. "Wanna come? There's some yummy coconut-lemon cake in here."

"Food? Real food and not camp slop?" Charity started licking her lips. "What are we waiting for, Mandy. Let's go."

Usually I hate being called anything except my full name—Amanda. But I didn't say anything about it because Charity has a nickname for all her friends.

Nobody was there when we got inside. Charity pushed Marietta's trunk in front of the door to block it.

"Why'd you do that?" I asked.

"We don't want to be interrupted until we get first crack at the really good stuff, do we?" Charity said, reaching for the box.

I hadn't thought of it like that, but it was a good idea. "Yeah," I said. Then I laughed to myself thinking how mad Marietta would get if she thought I had been using *her* trunk to keep *her* out.

Serves you right, Miss Alabama.

Charity was poking through the box. There were a lot of different things—small cookie tins, tin foil bundles, waxed-paper packages, and little jars with ribbons around them.

"Where's the fried chicken?" Charity asked, pulling back the tinfoil on one of the big bundles.

I wondered why Charity thought there would be fried chicken in the box. I hadn't said anything about having any. And why had she pronounced "fried chicken" like she had a southern accent? Weird.

The bundle she unwrapped was the coconut-lemon cake. "Shucks. No fried chicken," Charity said, using her weird southern-accent voice again. "Doesn't your godmother know what you like?"

I was trying to remember when I had told Charity that I

liked fried chicken. We had never even had it at Castle, although we did have chicken sometimes that wasn't fried. Maybe I had said something then?

I was just about to ask her when she opened one of the tin boxes. "Hmmm!" she said. "Chocolate-chip cookies. That's more like it."

Charity started gobbling up the cookies like she was starving. "Mandy," she said, "these are delicious! Your godmother knows her way around a kitchen!"

I took the two cookies Charity held out to me in her hand. I knew they were probably delicious like she said, but I didn't feel like eating them. All of a sudden I didn't feel like eating anything, not even the coconut-lemon cake.

Charity kept looking through the box, unwrapping and tasting everything. I sat there, not tasting anything, but Charity didn't seem to notice.

Finally everything was opened; no surprises were left. "Good stash, Man," Charity said, leaning back on the bed. "Your godmother's the best. That's enough stuff for a great lights-out party."

"Probably so," I said, wondering why I was beginning to feel sorrier and sorrier that Godmother Frankie had brought me anything at all.

Week 7

13 Ernestine

Hi, Jazz,

How's my favorite little sister? I won't even ask if you're having fun at Grandmother Carroll's because I already know you are. Mama wrote and told me that when she and Daddy talked to you on the phone, you asked if you could stay there until Christmas!

Since I know you're enjoying yourself, I don't mind telling you about camp. Remember when I said I would hate being here? Mama told me that before I made up my mind to really hate Hilltop, I should try to find ten good things about it. She said practically everything has something good in it. I found the ten things, and here they are. (I sent this list to Mama, too.)

1. Breakfast takes away my appetite. I only have juice because the eggs are runny and the oatmeal is gray, BUT, keep reading.

2. There's so much chlorine in the swimming pool, I'm beginning to smell like a water fountain, BUT I've learned how to swim! (My

friend Raelynn is teaching me and has been calling me Dolphin Girl for the past week!)

3. My art counselor is as cranky as a bear. BUT for art class I decided to make a statue of a bear (she calls it a bear sculpture) and use my counselor's face as the model for the bear's face.

4. Lunch takes away my appetite, so I only eat the lettuce and tomatoes. You can never tell what the meat is, and the potatoes are always burned or mushy. BUT keeep reading.

5. I hate softball, BUT I've found a great place to hide to get out of playing. It's a corner of Tubman Hall that they've turned into a library and where they keep a bunch of books about famous black people (like Tubman Hall is named after Harriet Tubman).

6. When we went on a six-mile nature hike, I got blisters on both of my heels, BUT I didn't get poison ivy like some of my friends did.

7. Dinner takes away my appetite. They always serve some kind of queer soup and things like cheese sandwiches. I only eat the fruit or pudding they have for dessert. BUT keeeep reading.

8. We aren't allowed to sing the best camp songs when the counselors are around, BUT we sing them anyhow after lights-out.

9. There are so many *RULES!* They have rules about when to get up, when to eat, when to swim, when to do everything! BUT, the mountain air is so great I fall asleep every night practically as soon as I lie down after lights-out.

10. Since all the hideous meals take away my appetite, I'VE LOST WEIGHT! Honest and truly, truly, truly! And there's no BUT about it!

Camp is fun, Jazz. Honest and truly. I'm going to start saving my money so that when you get old enough, you and I can come here together. Give Grandmother a big hug for me (I know how you hate kisses). See you soon (long before Christmas)!

Love,
Ernestine

By the time I finished my letter, it was after lights-out. My light was the last one on, but before I turned it off I had to check inside my bed to make sure nobody had short-sheeted it or stuffed bugs under the pillow. I had to do this every night. Especially since I lived in the same bunk room with Paulette Taylor, the champion of dirty-trick players at Hilltop.

I finished checking my bed and had just turned off the light when I heard the door to our bunk room creaking open.

Paulette, who had the bunk above mine, heard the creak the same time I did. "Who's that?" she said in a peculiar, fake deep voice.

Paulette is short and very tiny. Her voice is so little it's practically no more than a squeak, and she kinda keeps her head down when she's talking with anybody. When I first met Paulette I figured she was one of the shyest persons in the world. I figured *really* wrong. Paulette wasn't afraid to try anything and could practically get away with murder!

"I said, who's that?" Paulette said again. This time she tried to make her voice even deeper.

"It's me." It was Deena. I recognized her voice right away. "Is that you, Paulette?" she said. "Girl, if you tryin' to disguise your voice, you gotta do more than that."

"*Shhhh!*" a bunch of us said at the same time. Deena was a terrible whisperer. If Mrs. Williamson came by and heard her in our bunk room, everybody would get into trouble.

"What'chall worried about?" Deena said. She was almost speaking in her regular voice. "Nobody's gonna catch me in here. All the counselors are at a meeting over in Wheatley Pavilion. I know 'cause I heard Miss Rutherford talking to one of the J. C.s about it."

Deena practically threw herself down on my bunk. "Hey, homegirl," she said. "What's new?" It was shadow dark in our room, but I could feel her grin.

"Deena, I saw you practically an hour ago. How come you think somethin's new since then?"

"Somethin' could be," she said. "A lot can happen in an hour."

"Well, nothin' happened over here." I moved over in my bed to make room for Deena's long legs which she was stretching out near my pillow. Since they were practically in my face, I decided to sit up. "Did somethin' happen over your way?" I asked her.

"Nah." Deena decided to sit up, too, and rest her back against the bedpost. "Since I knew our bunk warden was in a meeting with all the rest of the wardens, I thought this would be a good night to make a lights-out run."

Warden. I haven't heard that word for ages. Not since Miss Elder's...

All of my thinking must have made me say something out loud without realizing it.

" 'Warden' what?" Deena was asking.

"Whadda you mean 'warden what'?" I said.

I could tell from Deena's shadow that she was putting her hands on her hips. "*You* said 'warden,'" she said, "then you didn't say nothin' else. Warden *what*?"

"Wow. I guess that's what people mean when they say they're thinking out loud!"

"Ernestine, what *are* you talkin' about?" Deena's shadow didn't show a frown, but I knew she had one on her face.

I still didn't think it was safe to talk too loud, so I leaned closer to Deena. "Hearing the word 'warden,'" I whispered, "made me think about somebody I know who used to call somebody else that we both know 'warden,' and I guess when I thought that, it made me say the word out loud without knowing that I was."

"*Huh?*"

Deena sounded so confused and speechless, I couldn't keep myself from laughing out loud.

"When you said 'warden,' it made me think of a girl I know," I said. "She and I take music lessons from the same person."

"Who?"

"Miss Elder. You know who I take music lessons from."

"Not your music teacher," Deena said. She wasn't even trying to whisper anymore. "Who's the girl you were thinking of."

"Oh," I said. "Amanda. Amanda Clay. She used to call Miss Elder's mother the warden."

"How come?"

It seemed like Deena's lights-out visit might go on forever, and I was getting sleepy. *Very* sleepy.

"It's a long story, Deena. I'll tell you about it another

time." I made my yawn big even though only a little one was ready to pop out.

Deena acted like she didn't even notice. "I never heard you talk about her," she said.

"You have so," I said. "I've told you a ton about Miss Elder."

"Not Miss Elder, girl," Deena said. "Amanda. You never told me about your friend Amanda."

"I didn't say she was my friend. I just said we take music lessons from the same person." I yawned again. This time I didn't have to pretend to do a big one.

"Look, Deena," I said. I lay back down. "I'll tell you about that stuff tomorrow. I'm really *really* sleepy now." I closed my eyes.

I could feel Deena getting up off the bed. "Next time I do a lights-out run, I'm not comin' here," she said. "It's too boring in here. I coulda had more fun stayin' in my own bunk."

"Hey, Deena, you think it's boring in here?"

Paulette's little mouse-voice was so full of giggles that my eyes popped open.

"I know what we can do so it won't be so boring," she said. "We can have a PILLOW FIGHT!" Paulette practically screamed the words.

Before anybody could say anything, a pillow hit Deena right in the face.

Right away, we all started grabbing pillows and looking for somebody to hit. We started chasing each other around the bunk room and screaming and laughing. *Everybody* forgot about it being after lights-out.

Jackie Lester had been jumping up and down on her top

bunk and clunking down her pillow on the head of anybody who came close. I guess her pillow was getting weaker and weaker because when she clunked me on the head, the pillow busted open!

Pillow feathers swirled everywhere! In the shadow dark it looked like falling clumps of gray-black snow. It would have been beautiful except that just as the picture was getting good in my mind, the door to our bunk room opened and the outline of Mrs. Williamson filled up the doorway.

"LADIES!"

We almost knocked each other out trying to get back into our beds before Mrs. Williamson could turn on the overhead light.

"I'm *surprrrrrrised* at you," Mrs. Williamson said. I could hear her long-fingernails-hand crawling over the walls, looking for the light switch. "And *verrrrry* disappointed." Then she found the switch and snapped on the light.

I had gotten back to my bed but only one leg had made it under the sheet. Deena was trying to roll under my bed but only her left side had made it.

Jackie had dived under her sheets but had gone head first. Beryl, Maxine, and Verdell were too far away from their beds to do anything but stand where they were and be guilty.

Only one person was where she should be. Under her sheet and blanket with her eyes fluttering like the light had woken her up. Sneaky, dirty-trick champion Paulette.

While I was trying to make myself invisible and get my entire body into the bed without anybody noticing, I could hear that squeaky, pretending-to-be-sleepy voice talking to Mrs. Williamson. "Wha...what's goin' on?" it said.

Boy, Paulette. One of these days you're gonna get it. You just wait. You'll see....

The words that popped into my thoughts made me think of Amanda again. And even though I knew I was in a whole bunch of trouble and *still* hadn't gotten my body all the way into my bed where it was supposed to be, I kinda felt like smiling.

14 Amanda

Dear Madelyn,

Camp Castle is terrific!!! I'm having a splashing time. Too bad you didn't go here like your friend Cynthia Morris did. You would have loved it, and then maybe I could have been an almost second generation Castle kid (ha ha). Some of my friends here really are generation Castle kids. That means their mothers or grandmothers went here.

Guess what? I've learned how to swim AND how to saddle a horse AND how to rig a sailboat—just in case you don't know, that means getting the boat ready to sail. I've only gone sailing a couple of times so far because I had to pass a swimming test before I could go out, but every time I've gone it's been splashing! And I'll be going a lot more before I come home.

You didn't say much in your letter about things at home. I think you were probably trying not to worry me. But ever since I talked with my friend Charity I haven't worried much anymore about the separation. Charity said her parents split when she was five years old and that it's a blast having two different homes. She said she gets twice as many presents and gets to go to twice as many terrific places—like on school vacations. Her parents finally got a divorce, but I don't think that will happen to Mother and Dad, do you? Anyway, while the separation is going on, maybe things won't be so bad for you and me.

There's lots more to tell you, but I've got to finish this letter and write to Mother. I already wrote to Dad. I'm asking each of them to send me something that can be our own special secret. I got the idea from Charity. Pretty clever, huh!

Hope you're having a little fun while you're working this summer (ha ha). Bye!

Love,
Amanda

After I finished Madelyn's letter, I decided to mail it right away so she would get it in time to write me back before I left camp. Maybe she'd even get the hint and send me something.

Castle had its own post office. It looked like a guard house and stood on the other side of the drawbridge. Sometimes the lady who worked behind the counter talked like she thought the post office *was* a real guard house and the camp was a real castle. She would say things like "An entire fortnight has passed since you lasses arrived at the gates." Weird.

While I was crossing the drawbridge on the way to the post office, I heard somebody calling my name. I looked around, but didn't see anybody behind or in front of me. Then I heard it again.

"Amanda! Down here."

The ground under the drawbridge curved down and led to the creek. I looked on both sides of the bridge and all along the creek, but I didn't see anybody anywhere.

"Amanda!"

This was really getting on my nerves. "Who's calling me?" I yelled.

"Look down. Straight down."

It felt weird to look straight down. Like I was expecting to see a drawbridge goblin or something. But when I looked through spaces between the wooden planks the bridge was made of, I *did* see somebody sitting right under the drawbridge.

"Leslie!"

"It sure took you long enough to find me," she said. "Where did you think the voice was coming from anyhow?"

After I jumped down to the ground, I had to crawl through the grass to fit under the bridge and get to where Leslie was sitting.

"I didn't expect to see anybody *under* the drawbridge," I said. I brushed off pieces of grass that had stuck to my hands and knees. "What are you tryin' to be sittin' here, a troll or something?"

Leslie made a face like she was a troll and giggled.

Sometimes being with Leslie reminded me of being with Alicia. Especially hearing her laugh.

"Sometimes I wish I *could* turn into a troll," she said.

Before I sat down next to Leslie, I looked up to make sure there weren't any spiders hanging from the bridge, since it was almost touching our heads. There weren't.

"No you wouldn't," I said. "Trolls are super ugly."

"How'd you know? You ever seen one?"

"Only Claudia Russell. She hasn't admitted that she's a troll, but she's ugly enough to be one."

"Amanda, that's mean," Leslie said, turning up her nose.

Sometimes Leslie reminded me so much of Alicia that it got on my nerves.

"How come you're sittin' down here?" I asked.

"Because it's one of my favorite places at Castle to be."

"It *is*?" I looked at Leslie, expecting to see her smiling. Like she had made a joke. But she looked serious.

"How come you like it here so much? It's cool and away from the sun and stuff, but it's mostly..." I wanted to say it was mostly *nothing*, but I didn't.

Leslie stared at the creek and picked at the grass without saying anything. Finally she said, "Because it's...private. Nobody comes here but me. I can be by myself and not have to explain why."

Then Leslie turned her head to look at me. "You won't tell anybody about this place, will you, Amanda?"

Why would anybody want to know in the first place?

I didn't say what I was thinking. I just asked, "Who would I tell?"

Leslie hunched her shoulders. "I don't know," she said. "Charity or somebody."

"I won't tell anybody," I said. And I knew I wouldn't. "But even if Charity found out by herself, she wouldn't say anything to anybody. Charity's cool."

Leslie didn't say anything, but she got a *look* on her face.

Alicia says I get looks on my face. One time last year after she had said what a nice person Ernestine Harris was and how I should get to know her, she said, "Why you gettin' that look on your face, Amanda?"

When I asked her what look she was talking about, she said, "Whenever I say something you don't want to hear or don't want to believe, you get that look on your face."

That night I had stood in front of the mirror and said inside my head, "Ernestine is a nice person." I stared at myself to see what look would come on my face, but I didn't notice anything different.

But sitting there looking at Leslie, I think I saw the look Alicia might have been talking about. A look that said she didn't believe what I was saying.

"How come you think Charity would tell about this place if she found out?" I asked.

"I didn't say she would," Leslie said.

"Yeah, but you got that look on your face," I said.

Leslie snatched up a handful of grass. "I don't know what look you're talkin' about," she said. "*I* don't think Charity's all that cool, but anyhow that's not the point."

"What *is* the point?"

Leslie looked at me again. This time it sorta reminded me of how Madelyn can look when she tries to explain something to me she thinks I'm too young or stupid to understand.

"Look, Amanda," Leslie said, "I just like comin' here and being by myself. Away from all of them."

Them?

Leslie kept brushing on the grass and talking. "Sometimes I just get tired of being around mostly white people all the time. Don't you?"

I really hadn't thought about it, but I didn't want Leslie giving me another one of her looks.

I hunched my shoulders. "It doesn't bother me," I said. "And anyway, everybody's treated the same, so why should it matter?"

"Is that what you *really* think?" Leslie said, giving me another look.

This was beginning to get on my nerves. "I *really* don't know what you're talkin' about, Leslie," I said. "All I know is that Castle is mostly a terrific camp. It would be nice if there were as many black girls here as white girls, but there aren't, so..."

"So...what?" Leslie said. She had stopped brushing the grass and was looking in my face.

"So, there just aren't," I said.

And that's that.

While she was brushing grass off her arm, Leslie looked at her watch. "Whoops! I didn't realize it was this late. I have a tennis lesson in five minutes. I gotta go!"

Leslie started crawling out from under the bridge. "See you at dinner," she said.

"Yeah," I said. "And, Leslie?"

She looked at me over her shoulder. "What?"

"Don't worry. I won't tell anybody about this place."

"Thanks, Amanda."

I could hear Leslie running across the bridge. After her footsteps disappeared, the only noise was the bubbling sound of the creek.

It is sort of nice here. Peaceful.

I thought some more about what Leslie had said.

Maybe she's thinking about people like Marietta Jarvis who treats people different just because they're black. But who cares. Marietta's a jerk anyway.

I wondered if Leslie would feel the same way if she were good friends with Charity like I was. Charity was one of the most popular girls at Castle, and she didn't treat me any different than she treated anybody else.

Thinking about Charity made me remember that we were supposed to go swimming together in the lagoon. She was going to teach me the scissors kick. It was almost the time we had said we would meet, and I still had to mail my letter.

I crawled from under the bridge in a hurry. But before I stood up to run to the guard-house post office, I looked in all directions to make sure nobody was around to see where I was coming from.

Don't worry, Leslie. It's a weird favorite place, but it'll be our secret. Our special black girl secret!

I felt myself smiling as I ran to mail my letter.

Week 8

15 Ernestine

"THIS WATER'S freezing!" I said, jerking my foot out of the pool.

"What'd you expect, bath water?" Raelynn grinned at me. She was finishing up her long braid. Her swimming hair style. "It's only six o'clock in the morning. The sun hasn't been out long enough to warm up the water."

"And it's not gonna be able to warm up me either," I said. I wrapped my towel around me. Putting my foot in that cold water made me shiver all over.

"You gonna let a little cool water hold you back?" Raelynn got up from the side of the pool where she had been sitting while she braided her hair. "No dolphin I know is afraid of a little cool water!"

Raelynn was coming toward me. I could tell by the look on her face that I'd better get out of the way fast. I figured right, but I moved too slow. She shoved me into the pool before I could get away.

"YIKES!"

"Better get outta my way, Dolphin Girl, 'cause I'm comin' in, too!" Raelynn yelled and then dove into the water.

"Com'on, Ernestine," she said. "Stop standin' there huddling up with yourself. Move. That'll warm you up."

I was so cold my teeth were chattering. It felt like I was even making the water vibrate.

"Harris, get a move on!"

Raelynn sounded so much like Miss Rutherford that I started moving without even thinking about it.

"Go on, Dolphin Girl," Raelynn yelled. "Do your swimming thing!"

Both of us started laughing.

Raelynn swam over to me. "Let's do a few laps together. We'll start off slow and easy before we heat it up." She winked. "Our speed, not the pool," she said.

After a few laps, we turned on our backs and floated a while. The water was still chilly, but I was beginning not to mind.

"I'm so proud of you, Dolphin Girl," Raelynn said. "You've worked hard and made all the effort pay off. You're stroking through this water like a pro!"

I knew there was a big dumb grin on my face, but I couldn't keep it inside.

"Did you have any idea when camp started that you'd be entering the swim meet?" she said.

"Are you kiddin'? I didn't even think I'd be able to float!" I said.

"It's hard to believe how well you've done," Raelynn said. She was kinda floating around me and I was doing the same around her. "Neidra says maybe you truly are part dolphin."

"No way," I said, laughing. "I'm all Morgan and Harris, although I bet nobody in my family is gonna believe how much I can swim when I tell them."

"Too bad you won't be able to show them when you get back home."

"Yeah."

Neither of us said anything, and for a while everything was quiet. It was just the two of us out in the pool. The water was a little ripply; the sun made it look like it had tiny jewels floating on top.

"What if I get too nervous?" I said.

"Too nervous for what?"

"Too nervous to remember how to swim."

Raelynn laughed. "Once you hit that water, your nervousness can't do anything but help you. It'll give you a rush of natural adrenaline to make you go faster."

She started paddling the water. "Go fast enough to win the meet!" she said, going in a faster circle.

Win the meet! The Hilltop junior division swim meet!

I began to get excited just thinking about it!

I turned over and started treading water. "Raelynn," I said, looking at her.

"Yeah?"

"If it weren't for you I wouldn't even be able to float," I said.

Raelynn floated right under my face. "What on earth are you talkin' about, little Dolphin?" she said. "Swimming is one of your gifts. It's something you were gonna be able to do, no matter what."

She turned over and came beside me. "Ready to get some serious practice in?" she said.

I nodded my head.

"Okay, then. Let's boogie!"

"On your mark, get set..."

"BRRRRRRR!"

When the whistle blew, I dove into the water. This time the cool water felt good as soon as I hit it.

There had been eight of us lined up along the edge of the pool. Each person had her own lane. Mine was the third from the left. But it was just like Raelynn had said. I didn't even notice the girls on either side of me. All I saw was the empty space in front of me. My water lane to the other end of the pool.

I could hear Raelynn's voice shouting to me. "Com'on, Dolphin Girl," she was saying. "Don't let those sharks catch up with you!"

For the first and fourth laps we had to do the crawl stroke. That was the stroke everybody learned as soon as they learned how to float and glide. It was the stroke I could do best. I pushed myself as hard as I could. Soon the tips of my fingers touched the wall of the other end of the pool.

One lap down. Three to go.

I pushed off and started doing the breast stroke. It was what we had to do for the second and third laps. It was an easy stroke to do, but it made me feel like I was going slow. Finally my fingers touched the wall again.

Two laps down. Two to go.

The second breast-stroke lap was harder then the first. I kept wanting to kick like you have to when you do the crawl so that I could move faster. I could hear Raelynn shouting at me.

"Keep it together, Dolphin Girl. You're doin' it!"

I could see the wall at the end of my water lane, but it seemed like forever before I touched it.

One more lap to go.

When I pushed off for the last lap, I could feel myself behind the girls on both sides of me.

Don't let them beat you!

I kicked and stroked as fast as I could. I shut my eyes so I wouldn't see anything. But I still heard Raelynn yelling.

"Com'on home, Ernestine. Com'on!"

When my fingers touched the wall, I was afraid to look anywhere. If I looked up, I knew I might see that somebody else had won and was already out of the pool. If I looked down, I was afraid I would see my heart floating down to the bottom of the pool. It was beating fast enough to push itself out of my body!

"Ernestine!"

I looked up. Raelynn was kneeling beside the pool above my lane. She had her hand out kinda like people do when they're ready to congratulate you.

"Did I win?"

Raelynn's smile was so big I almost didn't notice the way she was shaking her head.

"I didn't win."

"No, but you came in third."

"Third? Not even second?"

"A close third. Very close." Raelynn reached for my hand to help me out of the pool.

"Third's not close. It doesn't even count. It just means I lost. Really lost."

I didn't take Raelynn's hand and I didn't get out of the pool. I didn't even say anything. I just turned around and began to swim to the other end of the pool, doing the crawl one more time.

There was nobody left in the pool but me. The water felt cold and the chlorine was stinging my eyes like mad.

Dumb, dumb Ernestine. What made you think you could win a swim meet? What makes you think you could win anything?

I swam harder and harder, but the same thoughts kept popping into my head.

When I got out of the pool at the other end, I heard Raelynn calling me. I didn't answer.

And nobody wants a loser for a friend.

16 Amanda

THE BELLS AND gongs at Castle were getting on my nerves in a BIG way. The tower bell rang to wake us up and let us know when to go to bed (even though nobody ever went when it rang). And the meal gong outside the great hall got a pounding every day. Counselors hit it once for us to come into the dining hall, another for us to sit down, and another for us to be quiet and listen for announcements. Charity said that if Miss Prichard had her way, the gong would ring to tell everybody when to go to the bathroom.

On our way into the great hall for dinner, Leslie and I were talking about all the bells. "It's as bad as being back in school," I said. "It's almost making me glad camp will soon be over."

"I don't need anything to make *me* glad we'll be going home soon," Leslie said. "I miss being home with my family. Even with my kid brother, who's a nuisance most of the time."

"I miss my family, too," I said.

But I don't exactly miss being at home.

After the gong rang for the zillionth time and everybody at our table had been served, Kristen started talking about how excited we probably all were about the grand tournament.

"What's she talking about?" I asked Leslie.

"The big to-do they have every year near the end of camp," Leslie said, piling more potatoes on her plate. To be as skinny as she was, Leslie ate more than anybody I knew.

"It's mainly a bunch of contests," she said, globbing butter on her potatoes. "You know, swimming, sailing, archery, tennis, riding—everything. There'll be a contest for every activity they have at Castle. There's even a prize for the best decorated castle home."

"What did you say, Leslie?" Kristen asked. She knew we were talking together and not to anybody else at the table, but that's the way Kristen was. She tried to *make* people be a part of the whole group even when they weren't interested.

Leslie finished chewing before she said anything. "I was telling Amanda about the tournament."

"You haven't heard about the tournament?" Kristen said, in that oh, aren't-we-in-for-a-treat voice she has about everything at Castle.

"Everybody takes part in the grand tournament," Kristen said. "You'll love it."

Charity had reached across the table to get the milk, and her face was hidden from Kristen by the pitcher. "Yeah, Mandy," Charity said, crossing her eyes, "you'll simply *adore* it!"

Everybody who could see Charity's face laughed. And when Kristen said, "You certainly will," we laughed even harder.

"Who're you gonna vote for to be on the royal court, Kristen?" Charity asked, pouring milk in her glass.

"That's for me to know and you to find out," Kristen said, smiling and winking at Charity.

"Aren't you the sly one, Kristen," Charity said, smiling back at Kristen. But when Kristen turned around to say something to Candy, Charity made a face.

"What are they talking about—what's the royal court?" I asked Leslie. This time I really whispered so Kristen wouldn't butt in again.

"It's people chosen every year to rule over the grand tournament."

"Rule over?"

"You know, be the official starters of the contests, give out the prizes—stuff like that. No big deal." Leslie reached for more bread. "It's dumb, if you ask me."

"Who chooses the people?" I asked, hoping Leslie would answer before she stuffed the bread she was holding into her mouth. She didn't.

"Everybody," she said, finally. "Every castle home nominates one person for the ballot, and then everybody votes. The six girls who get the most votes get to be on the royal court."

"That's all?" I said. I was beginning to think Leslie was right. It *did* sound sorta dumb.

"Oh, yeah," Leslie said after she finished the last of her milk, "they take a picture of the royal court and put it in the newsletter, *Beyond the Drawbridge*. Everybody gets a copy when we get back home. It helps you remember stuff we did at Camp."

After Leslie poured herself some more milk, she said, "See the pictures on the wall behind the senior counselors' table?"

"Yeah?"

"They show all the royal courts. Every court Castle has had for every grand tournament they've ever had."

"So, being on the court is sorta like going down in history at Castle," I said.

Leslie looked at me over the rim of her milk glass. She had that look on her face again! But I didn't say anything about it this time. She didn't say anything else about the tournament either.

I didn't really care who would be nominated for the court from our castle home, but I was wondering about it while I walked over to see if Charity wanted to go to the movie they were having that night.

I bet she'll be the one nominated from her castle home. Everybody likes Charity.

I was taking the long way along the lake to get to Charity's home. It was my favorite place to walk at Castle. I liked it mostly when there wasn't anybody around but me and I could look at the big houses on the other side of the lake and pretend one of them was mine.

The best castle homes to stay in were the three nearest the lake. They were clumped together with the lake on one side and a bunch of trees on the other. Patricia Wilshure, who had lived in one of the lake castle homes every year she had been at Castle, said those houses stayed cool no matter how hot it got everywhere else.

When I come next year I want to stay in one of these.

I was turning down the lane leading away from the lake houses when I saw Charity going in the door of the castle home where Patricia lived. I started to yell to her, but decided to run over there instead.

I bet Patricia will be the one nominated from her home. She's rich enough to be real royalty!

I could hear Charity talking before I even got up to the door. "Patsy, you *got* to be kiddin' me!" she was saying.

"Nope, that's what she said."

The other person talking was Patricia. Even if Charity hadn't called her name, I would have known just by hearing the voice. Patricia always sounded like she was running out of breath.

I was on the step leading to the door when Charity said something else. "Well then, *she's* got to be kiddin'!" Charity laughed. "It would be ridiculous for Glory to be on the court!"

I stood still on the step. There was a funny tossing in my stomach. It was weird. Like one of my stomach organs had turned a flip or something. It happened exactly when Charity said Glory's name.

It was *very* weird because Glory wasn't one of my friends at Castle. I don't think we especially liked each other. Still...

I didn't put my hand on the doorknob or knock on the door, but I didn't turn around either. I just stood there on the step like I was frozen and kept listening to Charity and Patricia talk.

They wouldn't be sayin' anything if they knew I was here.

"Why not, Charity?" Patricia was saying. "Glory's cute and she has splashing clothes and—"

"And she's..." Charity cut Patricia off, but before she finished what she was saying, there was a loud noise like something fell on the floor.

"Think about it, Patsy," I heard Charity say after the noise. "We'd have somebody on the court named 'Glory'?" Charity's laugh sounded like a big out-of-tune bell. "Glory's parents probably meant to name her 'Gloria' but couldn't get that good old church song out of their minds—you know the one...'Mine eyes have seen the glory....' Or do you suppose their last name used to be 'Halleluia'?"

I felt the weird toss again. Only this time, it made me want to move. To get as far away as I could from Charity and Patricia and the lake castle homes. Away from a conversation I wished I had never been listening to in the first place.

I started running. Through the patches of trees and the grass fixed in the shapes of triangles and squares. Across the great Castle yard that men mowed and worked on every week. The "garden crew," Miss Pritchard called the men.

And all of the men are black.

I didn't stop running until I got to the tower. Then, without knowing why, I went inside and walked to the great hall.

Nobody was there. Everything from dinner had been cleaned up. All the chairs were piled up on the big round tables so the night crew could mop the floor like they did every night.

Everything is clean and put away. Mother would like it here.

I walked over to the wall where the photographs hung. It

was just like Leslie had said: Every picture showed the royal court. In each one there were six girls with crowns on their heads, sitting in chairs under a banner that read, "Grand Tournament." Every banner had a different year, beginning with 1905. And the girls in every single picture were white.

I began to feel like I had that first day at Castle. When it seemed that the pictures in the Castle brochure had come to life. Only now things were in reverse. Real life at Castle was turning into pictures instead of the other way around.

Camp Castle. It's a white people's camp all the way.

Although she wasn't in any of the photographs, all of a sudden a picture of Leslie's face came into my head. When I looked into that face that wasn't really there, I saw *that* look again, only this time I finally knew what it meant. And for the first time something that should have been weird wasn't weird at all.

Week 9

17 Ernestine

"HOW COME I can't get all this junk back in my suitcases? If I got it up here, I should be able to get it back home. Doesn't that make sense to you? I know my suitcase hasn't shrunk, so everything should fit. Maybe junk multiplies like rabbits. Wouldn't it be funny if it did..."

Deena had been talking forever. I had brought some of my things over to her bunk room so we could pack together. But with her mouth going nonstop, it was getting harder and harder for me to concentrate on what I was doing.

"You bought a Hilltop sweatshirt, didn't you, Ernestine? I did, too, but only one, and that's for my Mom. I got a size small because my mother, she's real tiny—remember how I told you we're always callin' her Little Mama just like we call our grandmother Big Mama. But one sweatshirt shouldn't, can't, take up all that much space...."

I can't even hear myself think!

"Deena!" I didn't want to cut her off, but I had to. "I just remembered something I gotta do. I'll be back in a little while." I grabbed the pile of clothes I had folded and practically ran out of the room.

Deena was one of the nicest girls I had ever met. She would do anything for a friend. I even hoped I would be able to see her once in a while when we got back home to Carey, but, whew! She could win a talking war without even trying!

I went into my bunk room, put the clothes on top of my suitcase, and looked around. I was almost all packed! Everything but my bed stuff and the clothes I was going to put on tomorrow. I figured it would be a good time for me to walk around and say good-bye to people. The buses were coming in the morning to take everybody home.

It was almost dark outside, but it didn't bother me. Not anymore. On my first day at Hilltop, I had dreaded night coming. The camp was so far away from everything. From houses and buildings and street lamps and other things that give off light no matter how late it is. There weren't even roads nearby where there'd be lights from passing cars and trucks. I decided that first day to make sure I was inside from the first minute of dark until the sun rose.

Now it was funny just remembering how I had been so afraid of the "still dark." That's what Mrs. Collins called the kind of nights we had at Hilltop. "Hilltop nights help you stay whole," she would say. "Up here on top of the mountain there's a still dark that helps you quiet things inside yourself and get close to them at the same time."

I was going to miss Mrs. Collins. Of all the counselors at Hilltop, she was my favorite. She took us into the woods for walks and explained a ton of things about nature. A couple of times we went for overnight hikes. Around the campfire Mrs. Collins would tell about things in the sky. Like about constellations. She helped us look for the constellation *Scorpius* which she said was very clear in the sky during the summer months. Deena said she could see the scorpion shape the stars made. I said I thought I could, but I don't think I ever really did.

Because of Mrs. Collins I had learned how to be really glad when the dark came. It was just like she said, "When the beautiful blackness wraps around us, it's easy to imagine that we're safe at the top of the world!"

I headed to Tubman Hall where I figured most of the kids who weren't packing would be. That's where the midnight campfire would be—the last camp event. It would actually be earlier than midnight, but that's what everyone called it.

I was in front of Tubman Hall when I heard someone call my name. I didn't have to wonder who it was. I recognized the voice right away: It was Raelynn.

When I turned around, Raelynn was almost right beside me. "Hey, Little Dolphin," she said, "I was beginning to think you had decided to swim far away out to sea."

I had felt horrible about the way I had acted after the swim meet. I had been so mad at myself for losing that I didn't want to talk to anybody—*especially* not to Raelynn, who had worked so hard to help me become a good swimmer.

After I had gotten out of the pool that day, I ran all the way into the woods near the softball field. I wanted to get away from everybody. I found a tree to sit under and stayed there until I got so shivery that I couldn't stand it anymore. I didn't even go to dinner that night. Just before the dinner call, I went to my bunk room and told our counselor I had a terrible headache and was going to bed. I did go, but for the first time ever at Hilltop, I couldn't go to sleep for hours.

I had been avoiding Raelynn ever since then. I had waved at her from a distance, but hadn't talked to her up close. And now there was nothing I could do but say something.

"Raelynn, I, ah," was all I could get out. Then I just stood there, probably looking more than a little dumb.

"Hmmm," Raelynn said, "even though it's not good to put words in somebody's mouth, maybe this time it'll be okay."

She started rubbing her chin with her thumb and fingers. The same way my uncle J. B. does sometimes when he's pulling on his beard.

"Let's see," Raelynn said, still rubbing, "you probably want to say that despite the fact you've become a good swimmer, you've also shown that you're not such a good sport, and *that* fact makes you feel very..."

She stopped rubbing and looked at me. I knew she wanted me to fill in the space. "Horrible. Horrendously horrible!" I said.

Raelynn kinda smiled, but she kept rubbing her chin.

"And the next time you enter a contest," she said, "you're going to try your very best to win. *But*, if you don't..."

"I won't be a sore loser," I said.

The way Raelynn stopped rubbing her chin and looked at me, I figured I had said the wrong thing.

"Ernestine," she said, "you really let me down."

"I know. Because I lost," I said.

"No, girl. Because you were a *sore* loser!"

"Raelynn, I—"

"'I' nothing," she said, putting her hands on her hips. "There's never an excuse for being a rotten loser, and if that's gonna be your attitude, don't get in the game."

I wanted to say "I'm sorry," but it sounded too lame even in my head.

Raelynn pushed my shoulder. "And you're too good *not* to be in the game, Dolphin Girl," she said. Her voice sounded regular again. Like she wasn't mad at me anymore.

"I'm sorry I…ah, acted like I did, Raelynn. It's just that I hated to lose the meet after you had worked so hard."

"*I* worked so hard? Get real, girl. You worked your bootie off! Why else would I be callin' you Dolphin Girl!" Raelynn smiled and winked at me. "Especially since you told me you didn't like being called 'Ernie'!"

It felt great to be standing there laughing with Raelynn. I was excited about going home and could hardly wait for tomorrow to come. But at the same time I knew I was going to miss her like crazy.

Raelynn looked at her watch. "I gotta start packing so I can come to the midnight campfire without any worries. You'll be there, right?"

"Yep," I said.

"Then we'll boogie later. See ya!" Raelynn waved and walked away.

Even if Raelynn hadn't been one of the greatest people I had ever met, I knew I would never forget her walk. It was so cool! I tried to memorize it while I watched her go to her bungalow.

She kinda twists her hips and shoulders at the same time and moves her arm like she's pushing air away from her body. Hmmm. I could probably do that, too, if I really tried....

18 Amanda

THIS TIME WHEN Godmother Frankie drove up to Castle, she came in a taxi. I was a little disappointed when I saw her, but only because I was hoping she would be in the convertible again. Especially since Patricia Wilshure was waiting there with me.

"Hey, Godchild!" Godmother waved out the window of the taxi as soon as she saw me.

"Where's the cool yellow car?" I asked after she got out and gave me a hug.

"With the cool man-friend it belongs to," she said, "and I'm not taking either one back to Carey with us."

Godmother laughed like she did when she had told a joke. I didn't get it, but I didn't say anything.

"Got all your stuff together, baby?" she asked.

"It's all here. I'm packed and ready to go."

I *was* ready to go. Things at Castle were beginning to get

on my nerves. Not everything, but enough to make me super ready to go home.

Ever since I had heard Charity talking that time when she didn't know I was listening, being around her had gotten really weird. It was like I wanted to say something and *didn't* want to say something at the same time. Whenever we were together, I felt like I acted different than I had before, but Charity acted the way she always had.

Like when she had seen me headed to the lake on the last day to go swimming. "Hey, Mandy, wait up!" Charity had yelled.

Hearing her call me 'Mandy' was getting on my nerves so bad I wanted to scream. But I still didn't say anything.

Soon I won't have to hear her call me anything.

"How come you didn't stop by to get me?" she said, popping me with her towel. "Don't you wanna finish learning how to do the scissors kick?"

"Uh-huh," I said. I kept looking at the ground.

"So, it's lucky for you I'm headed to the lake, too, wouldn't you say?"

Charity started whistling. I don't think she cared if I answered or not.

"Better hurry," she said, wrapping her towel around her neck. "Last one in the water is a big ugly frog!"

Charity took off running. I sorta ran, but not very hard. I didn't care if I was the last one in or not. When Charity got to the diving pier, she started chasing Kelly, laughing, and trying to push her into the lake.

I knew Charity didn't care, either, if I was the last one in or not. Charity didn't care, period.

I was glad Charity hadn't come up for breakfast the same time I did. The last morning at Castle was the only time we could come to a meal any time we wanted and sit anywhere there was a seat. It was because people were leaving at different times, and they wanted to make it easy for us to finish packing and say good-bye to our friends. It was also the last meal they would be serving.

I had brought my bags up when I came to get breakfast so I wouldn't have to go back to my castle home. Everybody but Marietta was gone anyhow, and I didn't care if I *ever* saw her again.

Patricia Wilshure came in and sat next to me at breakfast. She smiled and said "Hullo, Amanda," like she always did.

Even though Patricia was the one Charity had been talking to that day, I didn't feel weird being around her like I did Charity. In the first place, Patricia hadn't said anything... like what Charity said. And when Patricia found out she had been elected to the court (like everybody knew she would be) and Glory had come over to congratulate her, I heard her tell Glory that in her opinion all the court business was a little "silly." It seemed like she was trying to make Glory feel better because she knew Glory had wanted to be on the court.

"Somebody comin' to pick you up?" Patricia asked in her out-of-breath voice.

"My godmother," I said. "We're going home together on the train."

I wondered who would be picking Patricia up. Maybe it would be a limousine with a chauffeur. Marietta had been bragging about the limousine Patricia's mother had arrived in on Visitor's Day. Anybody would have thought it was Marietta's mother who had ridden up in it.

"Mummy's coming to pick me up," Patricia said. "Then we're flying to the Cape to meet Pops."

Maybe I'll get to the see the limo for myself.

Patricia had brought her stuff up before she came to breakfast the same way I had. So after breakfast we stayed together, waiting outside the tower. That's where we were when Godmother Frankie drove up.

I was glad Godmother would finally be able to meet Patricia. I had wanted to introduce them on Visitor's Day, but I hadn't seen Patricia while Godmother was still there.

Patricia shook Godmother's hand just like a grown-up would. "That's a splashing outfit, Mrs. Vines," she said.

Godmother got this big smile on her face. "That's a pretty splashing outfit you have on yourself, Patricia," she said.

The three of us stood there talking until Carolyn Medfield called Patricia to come over and say hello to her parents. Then, while the taxi man was stacking my suitcases into the trunk of the car, I saw Leslie headed to the tower. I yelled to her.

"Leslie, I thought you were leaving early this morning."

"I did, too," she said. "But Mama called late last night to say they wouldn't get here till this afternoon."

Leslie walked over to meet my godmother. "This is my friend, Leslie Mitchell," I said, introducing them.

"Leslie? Mitchell?" Godmother Frankie's eyes got super wide as she looked at Leslie.

"Yes, Ma'm," Leslie said.

"Are you Venice Mitchell's daughter?"

"Yes, Ma'm," Leslie said again.

"Leslie," Godmother said, and reached for Leslie's hand, "your mother and I were in school together. Only Venice's name was Morris then, not Mitchell. She became a Mitchell when she married your daddy, Casey."

"Yes, Ma'm," Leslie said for the third time. Only this time she was smiling as much as Godmother Frankie was while she was throwing her hands up in the air like she had found a bag of real diamonds.

"Leslie, I'm so happy to meet you. I've been hearing about you for years!" Godmother started hugging Leslie. I don't think she realized what she was doing, but Leslie didn't seem to mind.

"Where *is* your Mama?" Godmother asked, still holding onto Leslie. "I've been calling her for the last two weeks and haven't gotten any answer. I was hoping to see her before I left the area."

"She and Daddy went on vacation while I was here," Leslie said. "They're comin' back this afternoon and picking me up."

"Just my luck." Godmother sucked her teeth. "Our train leaves late this morning."

Godmother started asking Leslie a zillion questions. About her mother and father, where they lived now, how her mother liked her new job, where Leslie went to school, where Leslie's half-brother lived now...about everything. After talking to Leslie for only a few minutes, she knew more about her than *I* did.

"How long have you been coming here to camp?" Godmother wanted to know.

"This is only my second summer," Leslie said, "but I hope it'll be my last."

Godmother raised her eyebrows like she does sometimes when she hears something she thinks is interesting. "Oh?" she said, "why is that?"

Leslie hunched her shoulders. "Castle's okay, I guess," she said. "It's just that...I would just rather go somewhere else. Someplace like the camp Mama went to when she was my age."

"What kind of camp would that be, Leslie?" Godmother asked.

From the way Godmother's face looked, I think she thought she already knew the answer to the question.

"I'm not completely sure," Leslie said, "but for one thing there would probably be only black kids there."

Godmother didn't say anything, but her head was nodding. Very slowly.

"I mean, Castle is okay. It's really very nice," Leslie said. I could tell she didn't want to make it sound like Camp Castle was a bad place. "It's only...well, I think I'd like to be where I know that somebody likes me or *doesn't* like me because I'm *me*. You know, not because I'm black...or not black."

Godmother was still moving her head up and down in that slow way she had started doing while Leslie was explaining how she felt.

The weird thing was that I felt like I was doing the same thing.

But the weirdest of all were the pictures that kept coming into my head while I stood there listening to Leslie. Pictures of Ernestine! And the camp she had gone to. Hilltop. I don't know where the pictures came from because I didn't know anything about Hilltop. Only what Cynthia Morris had told me, and she hadn't said much. But even so, pictures of Hilltop were there. And they made me feel like it wasn't a bad place to be.

Ernestine and all her camper friends. Everybody's black.

Godmother put her arms around Leslie again. "Darlin'," she said, "you tell Venice for me that she has done herself one terrific job and has one lovely, young daughter."

Leslie smiled like I had never seen her do before. "Yes, Ma'm," she said.

"I would so like to hang around until they get here, but we've got a train to catch." Godmother picked up one of the two little bags that hadn't been stuffed in the trunk. "And this taxi is going to cost me a fortune!"

Leslie and I hugged good-bye. She hugged Godmother Frankie, too.

I'm going to miss Leslie. I wish we had done more things together than we did.

While our taxi was crossing over the drawbridge, I saw two people leaning against the guard-house post office. One of them was Charity.

The taxi window was open and when we passed by the two of them, I didn't even want to call out "good-bye." All I thought about doing was yelling, "MY NAME IS AMANDA, NOT MANDY! And don't you EVER forget it!" That's what I really wanted to do, but I didn't. I just kept looking straight ahead while the taxi rolled past the last of Camp Castle.

"So, Godchild, was it an adventure?" Godmother asked, putting her arm around my shoulders.

"Yeah," I said, leaning against her. "A real adventure. But I'm glad it's over."

I let out a long breath. It felt like one had been sitting in my chest, waiting to come out. It made me think of Madelyn and the long breaths she takes. Mother says it's Madelyn's way of being dramatic.

I can't believe it, but I'm actually going to be super happy to see Madelyn.

19 ❧ *Ernestine*

"BABY! Just look at you!"

Mama was holding both my shoulders like I was a dress she had taken out of her closet. But I didn't care. It felt so good to be close to her, I didn't care how she was holding me.

"Ernest, just look at our daughter. Our beautiful, *slimmed down* daughter!"

"I see, I see!" Daddy said. He wrapped his arms around me for one of his big daddy-bear hugs. "Buddy, you look terrific! I'd say that you and Hilltop were a magical mix."

I couldn't get the grin off my face even a little bit.

When the Hilltop bus had pulled into the parking lot next to Banneker, I think every girl on it felt the same way I did. All of us started rushing to get out as soon as the motor had stopped and the zwoosh sound opened the door. Deena and I were only two seats back from the driver, so we didn't have to wait long, but it had been hard to wait even a second! Both of us could see our parents standing in the parking lot, waiting for us.

After I hugged and kissed Mama and Daddy, I looked around to see who else was there. "Where's Jazz?" I asked. "Is she back yet?"

"Jazz'll be home tomorrow. She and Marcus both. He drove down to Grandmother Carroll's to get her," Daddy said.

Mama hadn't stopped looking at me since I got there. She was still grinning, but she was looking so *hard.*

"Is something wrong, Mama?"

"Why do you ask that, baby?" Mama said. The grin was still on her face.

"You keep lookin' at me. It seems to me like you're practically staring, Mama; and you tell us never to stare."

Mama started laughing. "I guess I *was* beginning to stare," she said, "but I can't help myself."

She rubbed her fingers along my cheek. "Ernestine," she said in a real soft voice, "in my eyes, my three children are the most beautiful in the world, but right now I can see that in the eyes of a whole lot more people than me, my Ernestine is going to be a real beauty!"

"Have mercy!" Daddy said, grinning just as big as Mama.

It was *great* being home!

By the time I had said good-bye to Deena and some of the other girls from Carey I had met, Mama and Daddy had packed all my stuff in the car and were ready to go. I kinda wanted to hang around a little longer and talk, but I was also anxious to tell Mama and Daddy everything about camp.

"I have so *much* to tell you," I said after we got on the road.

"We have some things to tell you, too," Mama said. She and Daddy looked at each other.

From their look I knew the news wasn't bad, and I didn't want to wait to hear it. "You first," I said.

"Just like it ought to be—age before beauty," Daddy said. "So here goes. I now have a part-time job at the university. I'll be working in the registrar's office."

"What's that?"

"That's where students' records are taken care of," Mama said. She turned around so she could look at me. "And one of the records your daddy will be taking care of in that office is his own!"

"Daddy! You started school just like you said."

I could see Daddy's face in the little mirror stuck on the windshield. He was grinning. "I'll be starting classes next month," he said.

"But Daddy, that means that every day you'll have to be in Logan where the university is." All of a sudden, this college stuff wasn't sounding all good.

"Not every day, baby. Daddy will be going to classes three days a week—" Mama started before Daddy cut her off.

"And working in the office those same three days. And on the other days I'll be a fixture in the house, watching every move my two girls even *think* about makin'!" Daddy winked into the little mirror where he knew I could see his face.

"That's okay, Daddy," I said. "We learned how to get around Mama, and we can get around you, too." I winked back at Daddy while he and Mama laughed with me.

I was thinking about Daddy driving to Logan three days a week when I remembered....

"Daddy! Mama! That's where my friend Raelynn lives. You know. The one who taught me how to swim and called me Dolphin Girl. I told you 'bout her in my letter."

Daddy looked at me through the mirror and Mama turned around again. "Raelynn lives in Logan?" Mama said.

"Yep. Her and Neidra, both."

"Neidra?"

"Neidra's Raelynn's best friend. They were both at Hilltop and both of 'em live in Logan." While I was explaining, I remembered something else.

"And you know what else, Daddy? Raelynn's dad works at the university, too! She said he was a...hue..." I thought for a minute to get it right. "A humanities professor! Yeah, that's it."

"What's Raelynn's last name, Buddy?"

"Jefferson."

"That must be Ray Jefferson's kid," Daddy said. He looked over at Mama. "You remember, Lou. I was tellin' you how I talked with him the other day when I was on campus."

"You know Raelynn's father?"

This is great! Maybe our whole families can get to be friends.

"If it's who we think it is, we know her mother, too. Linda Jefferson. Her family comes from around here."

"That's the one!" I said. "Raelynn's name is half her mom's and half her dad's. 'Ray,' 'Lin.' Get it? And, Mama, Raelynn is so nice. You'd just love her. Her hair is so long she can practically sit on it, but she's not one bit stuck up about it. And she took so much time with me—I mean she's practically sixteen, and she acted like she didn't mind at all takin' extra time to teach me how to be a good swimmer—"

"Sounds like this Raelynn made quite an impression on you," Mama said, rubbing her fingers on my cheek some more.

Daddy pulled into our driveway and I felt like laughing out loud. Our big, old, needing-paint house looked so great! I was home—*and* it seemed that some of the best parts of Hilltop might even go on. I might see Raelynn again, soon!

All of a sudden I couldn't wait to get inside. Maybe Mama had done something different in the house, like changed a room around. She had said she might put up new curtains in the dining room in time for my birthday party, which was coming up in two weeks!

As soon as Daddy cut off the motor, I opened the car door, popped out, and started running across the yard and up the porch steps, taking two at a time.

Week 10

20 Amanda

Dear Attorney Clay,

I can't come to lunch. Thank you for inviting me anyway. I hope you have a good meal.

Yours truly,
Amanda Clay

I read what I had written. It wasn't right, so I tore the letter up and started over.

Dear George,

Thank you for inviting me to have lunch with you, but I'm very busy and won't be able to come. When school starts I'll be even busier than I am now, so I don't know when I will be able to see you. Maybe I won't be too busy to see you next summer.

Sincerely,
Amanda

The letter still wasn't right, so I balled it up and took out another clean sheet of stationery. It was the last piece in the box, so I knew I'd have to get it right this time.

Dear Father,

I'm sorry I can't come to lunch, but I'm a little sick. I don't think it's anything serious, since my temperature keeps coming down. It was very high last night, almost 110 degrees, I think. But it's lower now, and that means I'm getting better. It's probably something I caught at camp. It may be the same thing two of the girls I lived with caught just before we had to leave to come home. One of them almost died, but both of them got better, finally. So my being sick is nothing you should worry about.

It's a good thing I won't be coming to lunch because every time I get close to food I throw up. But I know you'll have a good lunch anyhow with Madelyn.

Your other daughter,
Amanda

I read the letter three times to make sure it was right. Then I folded it and put it in one of the envelopes. There were a lot of them left.

I was about ready to take the letter to Madelyn when she knocked on my door. I knew it was her because of the soft knock and then the waiting for an answer. Whenever Mother knocks, her other hand is already on the doorknob, turning it to come in before she's even through knocking.

Dad always waited, too.

I started biting on my tongue again. The way I had been doing ever since the day I came back from Castle. That's when I found out that Dad had moved out. When he picked me and Godmother up at the train station and I asked why Mother hadn't come with him, he said that he had wanted some time to talk with me by myself. So after we dropped Godmother Frankie off at her house, we talked. But mostly him.

Dad told me he had moved out of our house to another one. The other house was closer to his office. When I asked him if that was the reason he moved, he just looked at me. For a long time. Then he said, "Amanda, you know the reason I moved. We've all been getting ourselves ready for this."

I haven't. I'll never ever, EVER be ready.

That's when I found out that biting my tongue kept me from crying. Sometimes it hurt so much when I bit it, I got tears in my eyes from being so mad about how it felt. But the pain tears never fell out of my eyes.

So, after I heard the knock on the door, I started biting my tongue so that I wouldn't cry when I gave the letter to Madelyn to give to Dad.

"Amanda," Madelyn said, "why aren't you ready?"

"Because I'm not going."

"Not going?"

"Are you hard of hearing?"

I waited for Madelyn to start fussing at me. But she didn't. She just stood there looking down at the floor. She even stopped frowning like she had started doing when I said I wasn't going.

"Okay, Amanda," she said finally. "Have it your way." She started pushing back her bangs that were part of her new hairstyle. "Do you want me to tell Dad anything?"

I held out the envelope. "Here's a letter I wrote for Dad. You won't have to tell him anything."

"Aren't you going to address the envelope?" she said.

"Why? It doesn't have to go in the mail. You're going to give it right to him, aren't you?"

"I still think you should write something on the envelope," Madelyn said. "You have time. I still have to brush my teeth. I'll be back after I finish."

After Madelyn left I looked at the envelope. It did look sorta weird with no name on it. So I wrote

George Clay, Esquire

Once I saw a letter for Dad that came in the mail with Esq. written after his name. When I asked him what it meant, he explained that it stood for "Esquire," which is a name used for lawyers. The name didn't look right for my letter, so I took out the letter and tore up the envelope. I got another envelope and wrote

George Clay, Father

It looked okay, so I put the letter in it for the last time and sealed up the envelope.

Since Madelyn had left the door open, she didn't have to knock when she came back. She walked in and stuck out her hand.

"Is it ready?" she asked.

I didn't say anything. I just handed her the letter.

Madelyn read what was on the envelope, but she didn't say anything about what I had written.

"Have a good lunch," I said.

Madelyn turned around to leave my bedroom. "Amanda, are you *sure* you won't change your mind?" she said through her turned back.

"I'm sure."

"And you're just gonna stay here with Mother and Grandmama Nelson?"

Our grandmother—Mother's mother—had been at our house when I got back from camp. She said she was only going to stay for a week or two, but it looked like she had brought enough clothes to stay for months.

Grandmama Nelson is nice enough, I guess, but I'm not really that close to her. She wears a lot of strong perfume and jewelry that clinks. Ever since I had come home, she mostly sat around with Mother, talking and drinking coffee. Whenever I came in the room, they would stop talking and smile at me and say something like, "Can I get you something, sweetheart?"

Neither Grandmama or Mother paid much attention to what I was doing. They probably wouldn't even know I hadn't gone to lunch if Madelyn didn't tell them.

"I need to go through my closet and see what new clothes I'm gonna need for school," I said to Madelyn's back.

Madelyn kept standing there, not saying anything. Finally she turned around. Her eyes were super shiny.

"Amanda," she said. Her voice was real quiet. "I have to bite my tongue a lot, too. And whenever I do, I also try hard to remember that I'm not alone. That I have you—someone who knows *exactly* how I feel because she feels that way, too."

Then Madelyn turned her back again. "You remember that, Amanda. Remember that every time you start biting *your* tongue."

After Madelyn closed the door behind her, I walked over to my closet. It has a sliding door that gets off the track sometimes, so I pushed the door open very slowly so it wouldn't slide off this time. Then I stepped inside the closet and slid it closed again the same way.

I sat on the closet floor. The buckles of the new patent leather shoes Grandmama Nelson brought me stuck me in my behind. I knew I was mooshing the shoes, but I didn't care.

I felt the tears coming from behind my head, so I started biting my tongue as hard as I could. But I knew it wouldn't help.

Nothing's ever gonna help.

I let the tears go ahead and wet up my face and my neck and my arms. They even fell into my ears. I started to pull down the blouse that was hanging over my head and use it as a hanky. But I didn't.

I just sat there and let the stupid tears fall and fall and fall.

I'll just keep sitting here and let out all the tears in my body.

Then I'll never have to bite my tongue again....

I might have sat there for the rest of my life if the telephone hadn't started ringing. It rang almost a zillion times before Mother finally answered it.

"Amanda," she called. "It's for you."

Maybe it's Dad. Maybe he's so worried about me he's decided to move back home.

"Be there in a minute, Mother!" I had to almost scream so she would be able to hear me all the way through the clothes and the closet door.

21 ❧ *Ernestine*

I FIGURED Clovis was joking when he said that I should call Amanda up on the telephone and invite her to my birthday party. "Clovis," I said, "give me *one* good reason why I should invite Amanda to my birthday party."

"She invited you to hers."

"That's not a *good* reason; that's a payback reason. And I shouldn't have to do any paybacks on my birthday."

Clovis started moving his head back and forth the same way his grandmother does. He does it all the time and I should have been used to it. But right then, it felt like he was doing it to be a pain on purpose.

"Whachu shaking your head like that for, boy?" I said. "The only people *anybody* should invite to their birthday party are the people they *want* to be there."

"Do you think that's why Amanda invited you to her party?" Clovis said. He was picking through the stones he had picked up from the flower bed Mama had planted beside our porch.

"I think Amanda invited me because of Alicia," I said. "I already told you that."

"Then, why don't you ask Alicia about inviting Amanda?" Clovis pitched one of the stones across the yard.

"Maybe I will," I said, getting up from the steps where we had been sitting. "I might as well ask somebody besides you, 'cause you're no help at all. You're just a pain!"

Clovis didn't even turn around. He just kept throwing the pebbles, one by one.

"And you better stop pitchin' all of Mama's pebbles into the street," I yelled back to Clovis before I slammed the screen door.

Sometimes I wonder why we're such good friends....

I was starting upstairs when the phone rang. It was Alicia.

"Girl, I was just thinkin' about callin' you," I said after she said hello.

"Any particular reason?"

"Yeah. Clovis thinks I should invite Amanda to my birthday party."

I waited for Alicia to laugh or to say "why" or to say *something*. But all I heard on the other end was silence.

"Hello? Is anybody there?"

"I'm still here," Alicia said.

More silence.

"Alicia—" I started, but then I got it.

"Alicia! You think I should invite Amanda just like Clovis does!" I was practically yelling in her ear, so I began to whisper in the phone.

"That's why you're not sayin' anything," I said. "You think I should invite Amanda to my birthday party just because she invited me to hers, don't you?"

I knew I should give Alicia time to answer, but I wanted her to know one more thing before she did, so I kept talking.

"But her inviting me isn't the same as me inviting her. Amanda's the one who's been evil to me. She's been like that plenty of times. Even at her own birthday party she was snooty. You know she was!"

My voice kept getting loud. "And I've *never* been evil to Amanda—not really. I mean, sometimes I wanted to say something to her. A couple of times I've even wanted to trip her up, but I've never really done anything, and you know it!"

I stopped so Alicia could hear silence on my end.

"Ernestine?" Alicia said. "Are you gettin' mad at *me*?"

Alicia's voice is real sweet. And it's not a fake sweet. Even if I had been getting mad, it would be hard to stay that way, listening to her voice.

"No," I said. "I just get kinda angry thinkin' about Amanda."

"Ernestine, I'm gonna tell you somethin'," Alicia said. "But I'm not tellin' you because I want to talk about Amanda or anything like that—I mean, I know how Amanda can be sometimes, but she's still my friend."

She's lucky to have any friends, especially you.

"Maybe knowing what's goin' on with her will make it easier to...well, like Mommy said, Amanda has a lot on her plate."

"Huh?"

I could hear Alicia taking a big breath. "Ernestine," she said, "Amanda's father has moved out of their house. Her parents will probably be getting a divorce."

A big "ah" popped out from my throat without me even knowing it was there.

A divorce. How awful! Even worse than awful!

"Alicia..." I couldn't think of anything to say.

"I know," Alicia said. "I don't know what to say, either."

There was silence on both ends of the phone.

"Stuff has been rotten for a long time over at their house," Alicia said. "I mean, her parents have been arguing with each other for months. I hear my parents talking about it, but whenever me or Edna comes close, they stop."

What do you do when your father leaves home? How can you see him?

"I'm not makin' excuses for Amanda," Alicia was saying, "but I know that she's been upset about this for ages. I know *I* would be?"

I'd probably want to die.

"I know she acts...well, a little hateful sometimes; but, just imagine how she must be feeling inside."

I can't even start *imagining how I would feel.*

I cut Alicia off. "You know what, Alicia," I said, "I gotta get off this phone. I'll call you back later, but right now I have another call I have to make."

There was silence again on Alicia's end, but I could almost hear her smiling.

"Talk to you later, Ernestine," she said.

Before I made my call I wanted to go to my bedroom where I had been headed when Alicia called. I had to try on something to see if I wanted to wear it for my birthday party.

The new thing Mama had added to me and Jazz's bedroom while we were away was a full-length mirror. She put it up on the back of the door.

I pulled out the Hilltop T-shirt I had bought for myself at camp. After I got home I had cut it off so that it was like the T-shirts Raelynn and Neidra had worn.

I took off my blouse and slipped the T-shirt over my head. Then I stood in front of my new mirror and looked at myself.

I *had* lost weight. Even Jazz had noticed. "Ernestine," she had said when she got back from Grandmother's, "now my arms can meet when I give you a hug!"

Jazz will always be peculiar.

But I hadn't lost enought weight to wear the cut-off T-shirt. If I wore it with my stomach poking out under it like it was, people might not know I had lost any weight at all. Especially Amanda, who I knew called me "fatso" behind my back.

I wasn't going to wear that T-shirt to my party, no matter what. Even if Amanda turned down my invitation and wasn't going to be there. I took off the shirt, put my blouse back on, and went downstairs to make the call.

Week 11

22 ❧ *Amanda*

ALICIA AND EDNA and I went to Ernestine's party together; Mrs. Raymond dropped us off. My mother said she would pick us up, but Mrs. Raymond said that was okay because after she finished shopping she wanted to stop in for a minute and chat with Mrs. Harris, Ernestine's mother.

Alicia's mother is friends with Ernestine's mother?

Things were getting weirder and weirder.

The first weird thing was Ernestine calling me in the first place. I couldn't believe it when I picked up the phone and heard her voice on the other end.

"Hello, can I speak to Amanda?" she said like she didn't recognize my voice. I knew who *she* was right away.

"This is Amanda," I said. "Hello, Ernestine."

"Amanda! You don't sound like yourself."

"Who do I sound like?"

"You sound kinda like you have, um, an accent or somethin'. You just don't sound like you, that's all."

"Well, you sound like you."

"That's how I'm supposed to sound."

We had only been on the phone a minute and she was already trying to get on my nerves.

"Look, Ernestine," I said, "did you call me up to have an argument?"

"No. I called to invite you to my birthday party. It's gonna be next Saturday."

Madelyn probably asked Marcus to tell Ernestine to invite me.

"Splashing!"

"What?"

"I said, 'Splashing.' "

"Girl, whadda you talkin' about?" she said, like I was speaking in a foreign language. "I didn't say nothin' about going swimming. Where would we be going swimming? It's a party. A *party* at my house."

"For your information, Ernestine, splashing means like, 'terrific.' You know, 'great idea.' Stuff like that. People say it all the time."

"I never heard anybody say it before."

Of course you haven't. You've never met anybody like Patricia Wilshure.

"So? That doesn't mean it's not somethin' people say," I said. "Anyhow, what you've never heard of would probably fill a zillion encyclopedias."

It sounded like Ernestine was taking a long breath. "Look, Amanda," she said, "do you want to come to my party or not?"

It'll be better than doing nothing, I guess. Better than spending my life in the closet.

"Like I said, 'Splashing!' And just to make doubly sure

you understand, that means 'yes.' What time does it start?"

"Three o'clock. And *don't* bring a bathing suit."

"Very funny."

"I just want to make doubly sure you know we won't be going swimming."

"For your information," I said, "I went swimming so much this summer it was beginning to get on my nerves. We swam every day at my camp."

"And, for your information, so did we. Sometimes I went swimming *twice* a day."

I started to say "so what," but I didn't. I just said, "You'll have to tell me about *your* camp some time."

"I will," she said, "and you'll have to tell me about *yours*...."

You bet I will....

After we hung up, I looked in the mirror in the hall next to the telephone. As awful as I had been feeling before the telephone had rung, there was a stupid grin on my face. I hadn't even felt it come there. Weird.

Ernestine's party was in her yard *and* in her house. It was everywhere. And there weren't just kids at the party—there were grownups too. A lot of them were her relatives. Like her uncle whose name is something like J. B. He is super fine. Alicia and I both thought so.

Ernestine met us at the door and started introducing us to everybody in sight. Alicia knew some of the kids and grownups. But Edna and I hardly knew anybody. Edna said Alicia had been over to Ernestine's a lot before Ernestine went away to camp.

She hardly ever comes over to my house anymore. I don't blame her though. Sometimes I wish I wasn't there either.

Ernestine's house is very big—it has three stories. Alicia said Ernestine's brother Marcus has the third floor all to himself and that it's mostly a big attic. But the house is also very old. The paint was peeling off in a lot of places.

A lot of the houses on this side of town are old. I hardly knew anybody who lived in the neighborhood. I'd only been there when I came to church with my godmother. That's where I had seen Ernestine the first time.

When Ernestine introduced me and Edna to her mother, Mrs. Harris hugged both of us just like she did Alicia.

"I've been hoping I'd get a chance to meet you," Mrs. Harris said after she hugged me. "We're all so fond of your sister, Madelyn."

Before we went outside, Mrs. Harris took us in the living room. She said she wanted us to meet some of Ernestine's family. Mostly there were grownups in there playing cards. Whist. They were laughing and slapping cards down like crazy.

"My dad says Whist is some serious fun," Edna said, laughing. "He has friends over all the time to play cards."

"In this family, we consider birthdays to be one of the grand blessings, where fun *must* be had by all," Mrs. Harris said. "If you find out that you're not having fun, come and find one of the Harrises. We'll make sure you enjoy yourself—even if we have to tie you down and make you!"

Mrs. Harris has one of those laughs that makes you want to laugh, too, when you hear it.

I can see why Alicia likes comin' over here.

Ernestine's yard is big just like her house, and for the party it was decorated all over. There were even balloons tied to the clothesline in the back. There was a barbecue grill in the back, too. Ernestine's father was cooking hamburgers and hot dogs and ribs on the grill. He said the ribs were for the adults, but he gave some to anybody who asked. Alicia got some and shared them with me. At first I didn't want to ask for any so Mr. Harris wouldn't think I was impolite. But they were so good I finally asked on my own. They were delicious!

There was a record player set up on a table near the back door. Some of the adults and little kids were dancing when we first came outside. Ernestine's sister was dancing *and* singing. For a little kid she can *really* sing. When she sang that song about a satin doll, just about everybody stood around her to listen. She was terrific.

Jazz is super cute. And not fat at all. She's almost skinny.

Too bad Ernestine didn't take after her.

We played a few games, but mostly everybody just laughed and talked and danced. After a while, everybody was dancing, even the kids our age. When Marcus came, Madelyn was with him, and the *three* of us danced together. It was stupid, but still fun.

It was almost dark when Mrs. Raymond said it was time to go home. Alicia begged to stay longer. I didn't say anything, but I wouldn't have minded staying if she had said okay.

Ernestine and her mother and father came over to Mrs. Raymond's car with us to thank us for coming and to say good-bye. Her parents had their arms around each other.

They stayed that way the whole time we backed out of the driveway and started down the street. They were still that way when we turned the corner.

Ernestine is lucky. She's still sorta fat, but she's super, super lucky.

I had decided that all in all, it had been a very good day. The first all-good day in a long time. And then Mrs. Raymond turned the corner to get to the bridge leading to the side of town where we live. That's when I saw the street sign: Lendall Street.

My father moved to a house on Lendall Street.

All of a sudden I was glad we would be home soon and the day would finally be over.

Week 12

23 ❧ *Ernestine*

"SO, DID YOU hate havin' Amanda at your party? Was she a real pain at your party like you said she'd be?" Clovis asked while he looked at me over the top of his glasses. As usual.

I could tell it was an I-told-you-so question, so I decided to ignore him. Besides, Amanda hadn't been a pain or not been a pain. She had just been there.

Actually, Amanda's not all that bad...when she's not being evil.

Clovis and I were sitting on Gramma Taylor's back porch listening to the night symphony. It had been raining so hard for the last few days we hadn't been able to be outside anywhere—even on one of our porches.

"There's only one thing about my birthday that I hate," I said. "When it's time for my birthday, it's almost time for school to start. Arrrgh!" I clutched my throat. "School begins in a week."

I looked over at Clovis. "Can you believe that summer's almost over?"

"I can believe it," Clovis said. "And I'm glad. It's been a terrible summer."

"Not for me, it hasn't," I said. But I said it soft and tried not to sound too happy because I knew that Clovis's visit in Georgia really hadn't been all that great.

"I'll be glad to get back to school," Clovis said, swatting at a moth. "Especially since we'll be going to Du Bois Elementary."

Clovis and me and all the kids where we lived went to Fourth Street Elementary which was right on the next street from my house. But Fourth Street only went up to fifth grade.

"I guess," I said, thinking about the long walk we'd have every day if we didn't want to take the school bus. "Du Bois is a lot bigger."

"And Alicia goes there," Clovis said, looking over his glasses again.

And Amanda.

Both Clovis and I sat there not saying anything. I knew he was wondering about things just like I was. I was wondering what it was going to be like, being in the same school with Alicia. And Amanda. And if sixth grade was going to be a lot different at Du Bois than fifth grade had been at Fourth Street. And about Daddy being away at Logan three days a week and Mama teaching all of the time instead of just every now and then. And about Marcus leaving for college.

How come things have to change so much all the time?

"I'm gonna hate sayin' good-bye to Marcus," I said, swatting at the same old dusty moth.

"Yeah," Clovis said.

One of the best things about having Clovis as an also-best-friend is knowing that he knows practically exactly how I'm feeling without me having to say much. Like while we were sitting there on the porch, I knew he knew how much I was going to miss Marcus. My only big brother.

"It's gonna be really peculiar not having him there to bug me about tryin' to listen to him on the phone and gettin' out the bathroom and stuff like that."

"He's not going to be gone forever," Clovis said. He was looking at me straight and not over his glasses.

"Yeah, I know, but it still won't be the same."

The symphony was really loud. I was thinking that maybe rain gives the bugs special energy. I started to say something about that to Clovis; then I decided I didn't want to interrupt the music. Or the quiet.

Maybe not everything changes. Maybe some things can just go on and on and on and on and…

24 ❧ *Amanda*

ON THE DAY Madelyn went to lunch with Dad, he took her by his new house. The house on Lendall Street. When he called later that night to see how I was feeling, he asked me if I thought I might feel up to having breakfast and then spending the rest of the day with him one day soon, just me and him. Since I wanted to see the house, too, I said I would.

We went to King Tut's for breakfast. It's a drive-in, but it's my favorite place to eat. When I said I wanted to order a hamburger and strawberry milkshake, I waited for Dad to say something. But the only thing he said was, did I think my body was strong enough to handle such hearty food so early in the day? When I said it was, he said fine and gave the order to the carhop.

I didn't think Dad and I would have much to say to each other, but he acted like we hadn't talked in a zillion years. He especially wanted to know more about Castle. I had told him some things when I first got home, but he said he wanted to know everything. About what I learned how to do, what I liked most, and the friends I had made. I told him about Leslie and Patricia, but I didn't mention Charity. I hadn't even liked thinking about her since I'd left Castle. Whenever I did, I felt myself getting sorta mad.

I started feeling that way when Dad asked how I had felt about being in an integrated situation. I didn't want to get into it, so I just said, "It was an adventure."

"Adventures can be good and bad," he said.

"Yep." That was all I said. Dad looked over at me, but he didn't say anything else about it, either.

After we finished eating, Dad said, "Are you ready to see my new digs?"

Dad lives in a place where I don't live.

I was sipping the last of my milkshake, so it was easy to just nod my head and not say anything. It was also easy to bite on the tip of my tongue without looking like I was.

It felt so weird to go in Dad's house. I think he felt strange, too. I could tell by the way he would say something about the house or something he had in it and then look at me. I think he was trying to act like it was no big deal—him being there and having only *his* own stuff. Not Mother's stuff or Madelyn's or mine. No family stuff anywhere. Just his.

I couldn't think of what I should say or do; so when Dad said, "Just make yourself at home, sweetheart," for about the zillionth time, I asked if he minded if I made a phone call. He told me to go ahead and to use the phone in the bedroom if I wanted more privacy. I did.

There were two photographs next to the phone on the

little table beside Dad's bed—one of me and one of Madelyn. I looked at them while I dialed Alicia's number.

"Hello?"

"Hi, Alicia. It's me."

"Amanda! I thought you were going out with your dad."

"I did, I mean, I'm still with him. I'm at...his...new house."

It sounded like I was practicing new words.

"Oh."

I knew Alicia wanted to ask a bunch of questions and that she wouldn't. Alicia's really nice that way. Knowing when *not* to say anything. But I decided to tell her anyway. Maybe it would be good practice.

"Dad's...new house is...it's sort of small, but it's okay. There are...two bedrooms and a separate den. Dad says Madelyn and I can use either the extra bedroom or the den when we come over. He said I'll probably want to use the den because that's where he's going to put the television."

"He's gonna get a television?" Alicia sounded excited. So far, her parents had refused to get one. Mother had said she was going to get one, but she hadn't yet.

"He said I could invite friends over for a sleep-over," I said. "Maybe I'll have a television party."

"That would be terrific!" Alicia said.

I was telling Alicia about the kitchen and breakfast nook and getting ready to tell her about the little garden when I heard her mother calling her.

"Amanda, I gotta go," Alicia said. "Mommy's taking me and Edna to get some shoes. I'll call you back later."

I gave Alicia the number and then we hung up.

I didn't feel like going back in the living room yet. I could hear Dad putting his books in the bookcases built in the wall on both sides of his mantel.

His mantel.

I turned so I could look out the window on the other side of Dad's bed. I could see the garden. Dad had told me about it while we were driving over to his house.

His house.

The people who rented the house before Dad had planted the garden. It looked like they had picked all the food, too. Everything was gone except a few tomatoes that were still hanging on the vines.

That garden's had an Ernestine attack.

After the thought passed through my mind, I wondered why it had. Ernestine wasn't all that fat anymore. I didn't think I would call her 'fatso' now....

But I wouldn't call her "thin-so" yet either!

Ernestine had been very nice to me at her birthday party. We hadn't spent that much time together; but whenever I saw her, she acted like she was glad I was there.

Nicer to me than I was to her at my party....

I remembered how Ernestine had thanked all of us for coming to her party and wondered if I had thanked her for inviting me.

It's not too late.

I picked up...Dad's phone to make the call.

Ernestine & Amanda

"HI, ERNESTINE. This is Amanda."

"I know who it is. Hi, Amanda."

"Hi. Are you busy?"

"I'm supposed to be helpin' my brother pack, but all he's doin' right now is dropping books and junk all over the floor, and I'm *not* helpin' him do that."

"Is that the noise I hear?"

"It *is* loud, isn't it? Mama'll probably be up here in a minute to yell at us."

"Your mom's nice."

"Yeah, but she can yell when she wants to. She was on her good behavior for my party."

"Your party was nice, too. Thanks for inviting me."

"That's okay. Did you have fun?"

"Mm-hmm. I had a good time."

"Alicia told me she did, too. Edna didn't really say much.

Do you think she enjoyed herself?"

"I know she did. While we were in the car goin' home, she talked about how much fun she had dancin' with Billy Carson."

"Edna likes *Billy Carson*?"

"Don't you go spreadin' that, Ernestine. And you *better* not say *I* said anything about it."

"Billy Carson's too peculiar to spread anything about. I can't believe *anybody* likes him."

"He's not all that bad. He's better than that Charles guy. A whole lot better."

"You talkin' about Charles Jackson? Girl, you need to get yourself some glasses. Charles Jackson is fine."

"Not to me he isn't."

"Well, he is to me. And to practically every other girl who goes to Fourth Street Elementary."

"Well, he won't be anything special at Du Bois."

"Betcha he will."

"Betcha he won't."

"Betcha he will."

"Ernestine, just wait. You'll see...."